THE
LAST BACHELOR

JAY McINERNEY

BLOOMSBURY

LONDON · BERLIN · NEW YORK

First published in Great Britain 2009

Bloomsbury Publishing, London, Berlin and New York

36 Soho Square, London W1D 3QY

A CIP catalogue record for this book is available from the British Library

ISBN 978 0 7475 9984 5
10 9 8 7 6 5 4 3 2 1

Typeset by Hewer Text UK Ltd, Edinburgh
Printed in Great Britain by Clays Ltd, St Ives plc

The paper this book is printed on is certified independently in accordance with the rules of
the FSC. It is ancient-forest friendly. The printer holds chain of custody

FSC
Mixed Sources
Product group from well-managed
forests and other controlled sources
www.fsc.org
Cert no. SGS - COC - 2061
www.fsc.org
© 1996 Forest Stewardship Council

www.bloomsbury.com/jaymcinerney

CONTENTS

Sleeping with Pigs

"Wait a minute," my shrink says. "Stop. Go back. Did you say *in the bed*?"

I nod cautiously. Actually, my mind was drifting off on a tangent. Even as I was droning on about my failed marriage, I was wondering, not for the first time, why she had a picture of John Lennon in her office and whether it was an Annie Liebowitz. You know, the one where he's in a sleeveless New York City T-shirt with his arms crossed.

"The pig was sleeping in the bed. With you. In the marital bed. With you and your wife."

"Well, yes," I say.

"You've been coming to me for more than a year, trying to come to terms with your guilt about the breakup of your marriage, and this is the first time it's occurred to you to mention that the pig was sleeping with you in the bed?"

I can see her point. I don't know why I didn't mention it before. It was actually a big point of contention at the time. On the other hand, I was behaving so badly by then that I didn't really feel I was in a position to make demands. Blythe used to have all kinds of jokes about sleeping with two pigs. No, actually, it was the same joke over and over. Plus, McSweeney's my surname and she liked to call me McSwine.

"Was this a nightly occurrence? How long did it go on?"

"Pretty much every night for a year or so. Two years maybe. Mostly at the end."

"And where did the pig sleep?"

"Between us."

"Between you. *In the bed*." Apparently, she wants to make sure she's clear on this point.

"Sometimes it would burrow under the covers and sleep down at the foot."

"Didn't you think this was relevant to our enterprise here? To the whole question of the fate of the marriage? That you were being asked to sleep with a pig between you? Am I safe in assuming this wasn't you idea?"

"Of course not." About this at least, I can be emphatic. "It was hers."

"And you didn't object?"

"Well, yeah, sometimes. In the beginning."

"And then?"

"Well, you get used to things."

She sighs and shakes her head. "I think we need to talk about this."

I can see her point. In retrospect, here, on the Upper West Side of New York, sitting in this book-lined office across from my shrink, who is literally and figuratively framed within a constellation of diplomas and portraits of Carl Jung, Hannah Arendt and Anna Freud, I can imagine how bizarre this sounds. Now that it's come up, I'm kind of amazed myself that I let my ex-wife talk me into sharing the bed with her potbellied pig. Over time almost any-thing can come to seem normal in the course of a marriage: food fetishes, sexual kinks, even in-laws. First you get talked into a pet pig, and the next thing you know it's sleeping with you.

"How did it get up on the bed?"

"She built a ramp. With carpeted steps."

"And you didn't think this was . . . unusual? And, in terms of your marriage, unhealthy? How did you manage to have sexual relations with a— How big was the pig?"

"By then? Hard to say, really. Too big to lift anyway. I threw my back out the last time I tried. Hundred and sixty, hundred and seventy pounds. About my weight. Plus, the shape's kind of awkward and it's not like they're going to hold still and stay quiet when you try to pick them up." Normally, her expression is pretty imperturb-able, but for the first time in our association I get the impression that she's looking at me like I'm a crazy person. "They're actually very clean," I add. "And they're smarter than dogs." I realize I'm quoting my ex. I can anticipate my shrink saying something to the effect that we were enabling each other in our respective fantasy worlds.

She nods slowly, drinking this in, and regarding me with what seems to me an air of wonder mixed with disappointment, as if she now has to reevaluate our relationship and start again from the beginning. It's the kind of expression that leads me to wonder whether psychiatrists ever fire their patients. I want to point out, in my defense, that her cat's purring away in my lap and she didn't seem to think there was anything weird about that.

"Well," she says. "We certainly have a lot to talk about next week, don't we?"

Having thought I was marrying a southern belle, I hadn't counted on getting Ellie May Clampitt in the bargain. I met her at one of the most fashionable watering holes in Manhattan, where she made an unconsciously grand, fashionably late entrance on the arm of a movie star. It was a birthday dinner for my friend Jackson Peavey, and the chair next to mine had been empty for half an hour. When I asked someone about my absent dinner partner and was told the seat belonged to Blythe, Jackson's aunt, I imagined a blue-haired southern dowager. I certainly wasn't prepared for the leggy, luminous blonde who finally alighted beside me with the ease of someone effortlessly mounting a horse. Though she has since denied it, I could've sworn the movie star leaned over and whispered, "See you later," as he took his leave. She should have been thoroughly daunting, except that somehow she wasn't.

"Hey there, Blythe Peavey, delighted to meet you. If I'd known what an excellent seat I had, I would've absolutely come sooner. That's a beautiful shirt. Is it linen? I love that color with your eyes. Have I missed any bon mots or bad behavior?"

She dispensed compliments with a liberality that would have seemed insincere in anyone I found less attractive and made me feel as if we were dining alone, tête-à-tête. She seemed to know quite a bit about me, which I found gratifying, considering how little there was to know at that early moment in my life, and what she didn't know, she seemed to be in a desperate hurry to learn. Eventually I admitted that I'd been expecting someone much older.

"My brother Johnson, Jackson's dad, is almost twenty years older than I am," she explained. "Jackson loves calling me 'Aunt Blythe,' which seemed funny when he was ten and I was twelve, but now that he's followed me to New York, I'm thinking of offering him lots of money to quit it."

Later she told a self-deprecating story about having lunch, in her early days in the city, with Leo Castelli and an artist named John something—she hadn't caught his entire name. She found him rather attractive and confessed to possibly flirting with him a bit, frequently repeating his name and touching his arm. The artist became more and more remote, until he finally said, "My dear, I've been called a john before, but never by a woman." Castelli later told her that she'd been flirting with Jasper Johns. "You can imagine," she said, "that I've never been able to show my face at a Castelli opening again, for fear of running into him."

I thought her story was a kind of wonderful spoof of the name-dropping that passed for anecdote in the world I was then aspiring to enter.

She slipped away around midnight, whispering that she hoped to see me again and disappearing at a raucous moment, so that I was the only one to actually observe her departure. I would learn later that this was her habitual strategy, that she didn't believe in saying goodbye.

After that, I followed her career as a girl about town, watching for her at parties and in the gossip columns. She was one of those women who conquered Manhattan for a few years, who seemed to be everywhere and to know everyone interesting, although even the most brilliant and articulate among her admirers had a hard time defining the qualities that made her so popular, in part because her greatest gift was the ability to reflect and magnify the attributes of those around her, particularly with men, a talent that was much rarer in New York than it was in Tennessee. She had a way of identifying and admiring the traits you liked most in yourself, no matter how recessive, so that as long as you were with her, you could imagine you were the person you most wanted to be. "Tony is the most extraordinarily talented tax accountant." "Roger has the most exquisite taste of any heterosexual in the city." "Collin was without a doubt the most popular man in Savannah before he chose to break a thousand hearts and move up north." She added to the collective sense of self-esteem. And though it wasn't obvious at the time, it became clear after she left that she wasn't terribly invested in the whole scene—and that was another aspect of her charm. Unlike the rest of us, her lack of vaulting ambition gave her an aura of grace. As it turned out, she was just visiting from another world. Several admirers tried to get her to stay. I knew of three spurned marriage proposals—from a publishing mogul, a playwright and a tennis player—and two book dedications.

One theory about Blythe's elusiveness, propounded by her nephew, was that she would never marry anyone while her father—a former Tennessee governor and doting domestic tyrant—was alive. I never met the man, but he left a big footprint on his native soil. In Nashville, a street and two buildings, including the tallest skyscraper, were named for him. As the president of the chamber of commerce, he'd gone up against the prohibitionist lobby to legalize restaurant alcohol sales, reaping a whirlwind of calumny and death threats; for more than a year, Blythe had been attended by full-time bodyguards. He had not approved of any of Blythe's suitors, Jackson told me, not even the English lord who'd brought him a present of matched Purdey shotguns. And he certainly wouldn't have approved of me. Another of her expatriate kinsmen speculated it was the death of her beloved brother in Vietnam that had made her so skittish about long-term attachments. At any rate, she left the city before anybody had a chance to get tired of her, and before she became coarsened by it or embittered by watching younger women take her place.

Blythe went home to Tennessee to care for her ailing parents, but she kept her apartment in the city and returned for brief visits every couple of months. I saw her at parties with a poet or a CEO, or, once, with a ridiculously good-looking guy who, she said, was a carpenter from Tennessee. One night, at a cocktail party in an Upper East Side penthouse, I stepped outside to smoke a cigarette and found Blythe standing alone, her blond hair billowing in the breeze from the river. Against the backdrop of the downtown skyline—with her head slightly tilted to the right, it looked as if she were leaning up against the Chrysler Building—she seemed like the embodiment of all my cosmopolitan fantasies.

"Well," she said, "you've certainly made good since I last saw you."

It was true. My first book had been a success and I was currently adapting it for the screen. Perhaps this emboldened me enough to ask her out, something I would have been too intimidated to do a few years earlier. I couldn't believe my good fortune, and not long after finding myself in her bed at the end of our third date, I proposed. Why she accepted me, having turned down so many others, I can't really say. Maybe it was because her father had died the year before, or maybe she'd just gotten tired of fleeing. Sometimes I think she agreed to my proposal on a whim, marriage being one of the few adventures she hadn't essayed. Or it's possible I was just at the right place at the right moment, standing beside her when the music stopped playing. At the time, I never really asked the question, being more than a little full of myself and my own success, but in retrospect, I have to wonder. Better-looking, more successful, richer and funnier men than I had failed to drag her to the altar.

A childhood friend of Blythe once dropped a clue that I didn't initially pay much attention to, saying that I reminded her of Blythe's deceased older brother. "I don't know what it is, something about your smile, the way you carry yourself. But damn if you didn't make me think of Jimmy just now. They were really close. Blythe was just devastated." Later, I cautiously tested this theory on my wife. We were in bed, flipping through the on-screen cable guide, looking for movies. *Platoon* was coming up on HBO.

"I never really thought about it," she said in response to my question. "I suppose it's possible. Maybe, subconsciously, you do remind me of Jimmy."

"Do you think about him often?" I asked.

"No, not very," she said.

"Really?"

"You know, one of the things I hate about the South is the backward-looking aspect, the obsessive dwelling on the past. Nostalgia is like our regional disease. All that longing for the lost cause, lost plantations, Dixie. All those odes to the Confederate dead. That was one of the things I wanted to get away from when I went north. I try not to look back. Ever."

After our City Hall wedding, we split our time between Manhattan, where I taught a spring semester workshop at Columbia, and Tennessee, where we bought an antebellum farmhouse outside Nashville with sagging wide-board floors, tilting barns and ragged pastures. Early on it became clear that she was happier on the farm than she was on Park Avenue. I came to think of her as Persephone, who stoically suffered her six months in Hades in exchange for another six in the sunlight of the surface world. Which would make me the king of the underworld.

For a long time I was happy enough with the contrast between our two worlds. After a decade in the city, I was ready for a change—and I was in love. Honestly, I would have followed her anywhere, although there was something particularly romantic for me, student of Faulkner and Welty that I was, about seeing her in her natural environment. For me, the South was mysterious and exotic, and the sense of nostalgia for a lost Eden, the deeply ingrained social hierarchies and the polite insincerity of public discourse were all endlessly intriguing. I studied the local population with the detachment of an anthropologist and the passionate intensity of a man attempting to decode the mysteries of his wife.

In those early days, Blythe's menagerie consisted of six cats, one of which deposited a dead bird on my chest the first morning I woke up in her bed. "A welcome offering," she said. "You should feel very honored." But once we moved to the farm, the animal population exploded, starting with goats, eventually five of them. Blythe left the table in the middle of a dinner party to check on the pregnant goat that was confined in the laundry room and returned forty minutes later, her white peasant blouse thoroughly stained with blood. "We have a new member of the household," she said, sitting down to resume her meal as if she'd just stepped out to go to the bathroom. "Topsy just gave birth to a fine young billy goat. What did I miss?"

The chickens came next, although the foxes eventually took care of those—except for the one clever enough to move in with the goats. Our first horse was adopted from the local polo club after it came up lame; she took the second, a stately black Tennessee walking horse, in trade for a Parker side-by-side shotgun inherited from her father.

I took to the role of country squire, even going so far as to buy a secondhand John Deere tractor with a bush hog in order to cut the fields myself. At times I could almost imagine leaving my life in the city forever. In the spring, before the heat became unendurable, we would sit on the back porch and observe the sunsets, which could be positively lurid across the back pasture. I would fix a pitcher of martinis and we'd sit and watch the horizon flare up pink and orange. The air was laced with the sweet herbal tang of fresh cut grass and horse manure and you could feel it grow cooler as the fireflies became visible in the failing light. If we lacked anything at all, it was hard for me to imagine what it might be. Blythe, however, had plans.

I would always claim later that the pig was foisted on me through trickery, particularly after it had just eaten an entire coq au vin, or destroyed a cashmere coat in search of the packet of cashews in my breast pocket. She'd talked before about getting a potbellied pig, but I'd quashed the idea, or so I thought. Her strategy was to buy one for the movie star, whose fortieth-birthday party we'd been invited to, and for some reason couldn't attend. So in our stead, Blythe sent a baby potbellied pig to the event—at the Beverly Wilshire, dressed in a bridal veil. The pig was presented to the movie star shortly after the cake and was a big hit, especially with his kids, who apparently were pretty upset when he decided he couldn't keep it; he was about to go off on location for three months and his ex-wife wanted nothing to do with a pig, potbellied or otherwise. I think Blythe had been counting on this all along. In her birthday note she offered to raise the foundling if it didn't prove convenient for him to do so. A week later the pig was back in Tennessee.

If I'd known it was meant to be an indoor pet, I might have protested from the start, but in its infancy, when it was about the size of a football, it had the inherent charm of all baby mammals, and the fact that it was so easily trained to use a litter box was an added bonus. But somehow I assumed that when it got bigger and fatter, it would take its place outdoors with the other farmyard creatures as God and nature had intended. At any rate, I was led to believe that it would always remain a shrimp among pigs. "Potbellies don't get really big," Blythe assured me. "She's definitely fully grown," she said, a few months later, when she was already too heavy for Blythe to lift. "No way will she get any bigger than this. The breeder showed me pictures of her parents."

I don't quite know what compelled Blythe to surround herself with animals, even in the face of fierce and protracted human opposition. After two miscarriages and one round of in-vitro fertilization, we had both resigned ourselves to the fact that we weren't going to have children. This certainly played a role, but I think it was a preexisting condition. Her friends told me about the raccoons and squirrels of her childhood, and a previous boyfriend, with whom she was still on good terms, confided to me one night over bourbon that he thought she cared more about animals than people. At any rate, a week after Sweetheart arrived, Blythe discovered she was pregnant again. We might have been spared the pig if our son had been born a little earlier.

The pig was, if anything, cuter at first than the baby. Blythe certainly thought so. For three months after Dylan came home from the hospital, after a long bout with a staph infection, she seemed strangely indifferent to him, and far more absorbed by the piglet. Eventually her maternal impulses kicked in, for which I was grateful, although our sex life never really recovered. We would hardly have been the first couple to have experienced postpartum celibacy, but I couldn't help wondering if the pig, by now sleeping in a little box beside our bed, didn't bear some of the blame. Dylan gradually grew hair and developed recognizable human features, while Sweetheart, whom Blythe referred to as his older sister, soon sported long black bristles and a vast sagging belly. To me, she resembled a boar who'd come in from the wild in order to live the good life. I don't think it was ever Blythe's intention that her name would seem ironic, but it was hard not to see it as such.

Many of our friends were horrified once the pig got big enough to knock them over if they happened to be standing between it and a food source, or after it rooted through their purses or their luggage to snack on soaps and cosmetics. It didn't help that Blythe would inevitably blame the victims.

"Well, you could hardly expect a red-blooded pig to resist a delicious and highly aromatic Cadbury bar that just happened to be lying within easy reach, practically begging to be eaten. It's not fair. Really, Karen, you should watch where you leave your purse. Now she's going to have a tummy ache all night."

Pity the houseguest who made the mistake of leaving his suitcase on the floor and then tried to complain about the destruction. "You don't have to tell *me* she ate your prescriptions—she's been up all night puking her guts out. What the hell kind of pills did you bring into this house anyway? You could have killed little Sweetheart McSwine."

The houseguest would be too flabbergasted to point out that there was nothing little about Sweetheart, too flummoxed by Blythe's righteousness to press his grievance— the fact that hundreds of dollars of pharmaceuticals were consumed and that he would be suffering from acid reflux, insomnia, high cholestorol and high anxiety until he could replace them. Instead, he stammered an apology. He came from across the seas, after all; he'd heard about the eccentricity of southerners.

Blythe used to say pigs were smarter than dogs, and this one certainly showed great ingenuity in the pursuit of anything edible. Sweetheart learned to open the refrigerator door before her first birthday. She would feign sleep, only to lunge at a bag of potato chips or a bowl of popcorn when she sensed we'd let our guard down. Dylan was regularly robbed of his snacks and his bottle. If we failed to clear the table after a dinner party, she would inevitably pull the tablecloth to the floor in order to get at the leftovers. On the first such occasion we lost a fair portion of the antique crystal and china that Blythe had inherited from her parents. We heard the crash and went running downstairs from our bed—neither the first nor the last time the pig would interrupt coitus.

She was busy rooting in the remains of the cheese plate, becoming frenzied as Blythe tried to separate her from the feast, snorting and grunting as she engaged in a tug-of-war for the last of the Manchego. Then she bolted for the living room, sliding and nearly falling over as her hooves hit the bare floor beyond the dining-room carpet as Blythe jumped to her feet empty-handed. "Bad Sweetheart," she shouted. "Bad girl!"

"I don't believe this," I said, surveying the wreckage—the shards of Waterford and Worcester, the linen table-cloth soaked in red wine.

"Cheese is just so bad for her," she said.

"That's your big concern? That cheese is bad for her?"

"Well," she said, "at least there wasn't any chocolate on the table."

It was trying enough to have the pig in the house in Tennessee; weirder still when Blythe decided it should go with us to New York. She felt Sweetheart would be too lonely in Tennessee for six months without us. During our New York sojourns, we lived in one of the snottier co-op apartment buildings on the Upper East Side, where capital was only the most obvious of the entry requirements, and I certainly wouldn't have passed the co-op board if not for Blythe's venerable family name, which even graced the Declaration of Independence. I still couldn't believe they'd let me in, but I was pretty sure they'd draw the line at Sweetheart. "What they don't know won't hurt them," Blythe told me.

I pointed out the impracticality of transport, of sneaking Sweetheart into the building and keeping her existence a secret, but it was no use.

Blythe had a friend who designed handbags, and she had him construct a special carrying case with a sturdy plywood bottom. "She has to fly in the cabin with us," she insisted. "She'll be traumatized flying in the hold." I said that even if Sweetheart could fit under the seat, which I doubted, it was probably illegal to take a pig into the cabin of a passenger plane. "Then we'll just have to smuggle her aboard," she said.

Because the beast was now tipping the scales at eighty pounds, this scheme required my participation. On the morning of our departure, I staggered into the Nashville airport carrying a heavily reinforced black canvas shoulder bag. Blythe was carrying Dylan, who then weighed about eighteen pounds.

"What's in the bag?" the guard asked at the security checkpoint.

"Actually, it's a potbellied pig," Blythe said.

"A what?"

The other guards gathered around, more excited than alarmed, while I unzipped the front of the bag and Blythe expounded on the habits of the domestic pig.

"They're actually very clean. She loves to eat soap; she had a bar of Crabtree & Evelyn lemon verbena that she relished the other morning. A free-range pig will always go to the far corner of her enclosure to do her business, and Sweetheart has a litter box. . . . Well, yes, it's a big litter box. They eat just about anything, but we try to keep her on a vegetarian diet to help her retain her girlish figure."

In the end, the security supervisor couldn't recall any official ban on pigs, and Sweetheart marched through the metal detector on her leash while her bag went through the X-ray machine. A small crowd had gathered before we managed to stuff her back in her bag.

Blythe was addressing a young brother and sister. "Of course she knows her name. They're very smart—way smarter than dogs."

With no small difficulty, I hoisted the bag up on my shoulder and started toward the gate, moving deliberately, like a conscientious drunk. When our group number was called, I threw a jacket over my bulging carry-on and followed Blythe past the stewardess checking boarding passes—hoping Dylan might distract her—and lurched into the plane, located our seats and swung the bag into the space in front of them, though it didn't quite fit and its occupant was grunting indignantly. When I straightened up, I felt the sharp bite of a pulled muscle in my lower back. I pressed the top of the bag, the pig squealing away, and finally slid it under the seats. Glaring at my wife, who was standing in the aisle behind me, I indicated the window seat. She climbed in and perched, her feet resting on the bag; I eased myself into the aisle seat, grunting as I felt the hot stab of back pain. I'd just settled in beside her when a fat woman clutching a violin case tapped my shoulder. "I'm sorry, but I think this is my row. Twelve A. That would be the window seat."

"This is row thirteen," I said.

She pointed to the illuminated number over my head. "Twelve, see? You're in the next row back."

"Oh shit," I said, rolling my eyes and glaring at Blythe, who seemed to find the whole situation hysterically funny. From a certain point of view, I guess, it was funny. But from seat 12B, it was incredibly frustrating. It wasn't the pig, per se, although that was a major component. A year ago, even a month ago, I'd shared a frame of reference with Blythe; we lived within the same marriage. Her idiosyncrasies were charming and her faults, in the early years of our marriage, virtues. That she insisted on living with a pig and treating it like a member of the family was amusing enough, especially when we were still having sex on a regular basis. But now for the first time I felt myself looking over at her as if from a great distance, from outside the rosy bubble of our shared existence. At that moment I think I felt something turn cold inside of me.

With an almost palpable sigh of relief, I resumed my life in New York. For the next six months I was back on my own turf, among my friends arriving in a beautiful apartment, which I now shared with a potbellied pig—a pig that, by the end of the year, was well over a hundred pounds and far too big to be lifted. Blythe had taken one of the doormen into her confidence, but we had to hide her from our fellow shareholders and especially the super, a cranky tyrant who certainly would have reported us to the board. To prevent her detection, Blythe designed a secret compartment underneath the platform bed, where Sweetheart could be hidden on short notice.

As she grew, we had to get increasingly bigger litter boxes, which we concealed beneath a round side table draped in a floor-length cloth. Our occasional dinner parties would sometimes be interrupted by the thunder of hooves on the parquet as a black shape shot across the floor, disappeared under the table and then, after a pause, unleashed a hissing torrent. The contents of the litter box became something of an obsession for Blythe. Because our garbage was sorted by the super and his minions down in the basement, she believed it had to be disposed of outside the building. She solicited her friends and kept a collection of shopping bags—Barneys, Bergdorf, Chanel, Armani—

that would seem appropriate on the arm of an uptown girl, and once a day she would venture out with one of these, a beautiful woman carrying a bag of pig shit out to Park Avenue. She chose a different street-corner trash receptacle each day, fearing, irrationally, that the garbage collectors might become suspicious of agricultural waste and locate the illegal animal unless extraordinary measures of concealment were taken.

Blythe had her Sweetheart and I found mine.

With her I could talk about how I felt underappreciated and unsatisfied at home; many were the justifications with which I mollified my conscience, although the pig wasn't necessarily one of them. To me, it was now merely a fact of life, albeit one that signaled Blythe's increasing distance from social conventions, especially as practiced on the island of Manhattan. Whatever the rationalizations for my affair, it would hardly have been possible if Blythe hadn't grown increasingly withdrawn, frequently sending me off into the night on my own while she stayed in the apartment with Dylan and Sweetheart and her needle-point.

After all those years of being a virtual dervish, Blythe seemed to have lost her curiosity. "I think I've already been to that party," she would say when I would run an invitation past her. "Like about three thousand times." I don't know, maybe we're all born with certain quotas and she'd hit her limit of parties. A jaded fried of mine likes to say that God allows us all a swimming pool full of vodka and a bathtub full of cocaine, and that he finally quit the latter after realizing he'd started in on his second bathtub.

Blythe had burned pretty bright and steady in her early days in New York. Maybe some filament had burned out. She'd gone to more parties, on the arms of more men, than most people even read about in the course of their lifetimes.

She preferred to sit on the couch, a bowl of popcorn within reach on the coffee table, reading a book, one foot rubbing the belly of the pig lying beneath her, our son crawling around on the floor. "Besides, somebody has to watch Dylan." I pointed out that we had a nanny to watch Dylan, not to mention that he'd be asleep anyway by the time the party started. "Well, somebody has to watch Sweetheart."

Perhaps she'd evolved to a higher plane of consciousness and no longer required the shallow distractions of small talk and flirtation, of voyeurism and self-display. But I did and I wasn't ready to retire. Even though I'd sworn off the bathtub, I still had several feet of vodka left in my swimming pool and I was still drawn to the music of the night. And inevitably I was drawn to a face across the room, the glance that kindled the flash of a provocative smile.

My affair with Katrina lasted for the duration of that Manhattan sojourn, almost six months. It seemed incredible that Blythe didn't question me more closely about my late nights and midday disappearances. With each successful tryst, I became more emboldened, more entitled, less guilty about my transgression. I didn't really have a plan or a specific ambition for the affair. Katrina was funny and sexy, and she also seemed to be happy with a part-time lover, with the stolen hours and midnight departures. I often went to sleep on the daybed in my office so as not to wake Blythe and Sweetheart, although I would often, after a late night, return to the master bedroom for a restorative nap; on these occasions, Sweetheart liked to join me, shoving her nose into my armpit and stabbing me with her hooves. Actually, it was strange how well we got along during this period, after almost two years of uneasy coexistence.

Katrina and I had been friends for years, a fact that helped to mask the drift into physical intimacy, to make it seem innocent even to ourselves, right up until the irrevocable moment—the kiss in the back of the taxi, my hand sliding down her shoulder to her breast, her hand sliding up my knee.

"This is probably a terrible idea," Katrina said as she unfastened my belt. After the night we moved from her couch to her bed, we fell into a pattern of twice-a-week trysts.

I probably would've been satisfied with this arrangement indefinitely, but eventually Katrina's conscience started to bother her; she wanted more, yet was loathe to demand it, and I wasn't nearly ready to leave Blythe. But I was crushed when Katrina ended our affair, and in order to console myself, I embarked on a crime spree of serial infidelities. Or perhaps I'm being too easy on myself; maybe I'd just developed a taste for it.

I must have been exuding some kind of scent that telegraphed my debauched availability and my intentions, because there were willing women wherever I looked. I had never noticed them in the early years of my marriage, but suddenly I was awash in opportunity: the dental assistant who held my gaze as she suctioned my gums; the librarian who helped me find Peter Quennell's *Byron in Italy*; the studio executive I met on the plane to L.A. I was compulsive and insatiable. It reminded me of one of Blythe's folksier aphorisms—that once a dog starts sucking eggs, there's no stopping him. In her part of the world, where guns were standard household equipment, the implication was that the dog needed to be shot. Yet in the end she was surprisingly forgiving.

The tipping point was reached back in Tennessee, where I was spotted emerging from a hotel at midnight with the wife of one of Blythe's cousins. At that point, the community, which teemed with friends and relatives, took it upon itself to advise Blythe that enough was enough.

The showdown was surprisingly muted.

We were lying in bed, Sweetheart splayed between us, her sharp cloven hoofs thrust toward me. She grunted interrogatively, hoping for a tummy rub, just as Blythe launched her interrogation.

"They say people are calling me the Hillary Clinton of Tennessee."

Scared and guilty as I was that we were finally addressing the elephant in the room, I tried to delay the inevitable. "Down here, I guess that's a bad thing to be."

"This isn't the time for you to be a smart-ass Yankee. They mean I'm a fool who's turning a blind eye to your flagrant and relentless philandering."

"I know," I said. I was, I realized, actually relieved that we were finally discussing this.

"This can't go on. I can't go on."

"I know."

"You realize my father would have had you shot. And I'm not even exaggerating."

"I guess I could only say I deserve it."

"Now you're exaggerating. You don't believe that, so stop bullshitting me. Stop bullshitting yourself. You've been lying to both of us. And don't you dare say *not really*. Not telling isn't the same as not lying. Now listen, I'm not going to give you a real hard time about this, though I probably should. People think I'm crazy, that I should cut your balls off and have done with it, but I just don't have it in me to yell and scream and cuss. I can't say I'm not hurt. I am. You really stabbed me in the heart and turned the blade. But nobody can help falling out of love with someone else."

"It's not that," I said. "I still—"

"Shut up and listen," she said. "All I ask is that you tell me everything—and everyone. I'm serious about this. You owe me that much at least. And if I think you're not being honest, you'll end up wishing Daddy was still around to shoot you and put you out of you misery."

So, I told her. About Katrina. About the dental assistant and the librarian and the studio executive, about her cousin-in-law and the neighbor two farms down who'd come over to dinner one night and flirted across the table, then ridden her horse over a couple days later after seeing Blythe drive into town.

"That sneaky cunt! Goddamn her. I saw her shaking her cleavage under your nose. But I hardly thought she'd come riding right over here like Annie Oakley and fuck my husband."

It was curious how she seemed to blame the women more than me; she hated every one of them from that day forward. I have no idea why I largely escaped blame. It was like the time when Sweetheart ate our houseguest's Dopp kit. She didn't find fault with me so much as with the women who'd tempted me, who'd waved treats in front of my face. Over the years she managed to cut most of them dead, to let them know that *she* knew and was pissed. This is another southern trait—cutting people—and she's good at it. She didn't forgive and she didn't forget, except in the case of Katrina, who, she felt, had at least shown remorse and done the right thing by breaking up with me. Years later, at a play opening in New York, she went out of her way to let her know that it was okay. As to her treatment of me, I eventually remembered the conversation we'd had about her brother, when she'd said she never looked back.

Even by her own admission, Blythe's post-marital dating life was somewhat compromised by the presence of Sweetheart. "I've become familiar with a certain facial expression," she told me. "These guys walk in and look at Sweetheart and what they're wondering is, *How long does a pig live?* They're wondering if they can outlast her. Sometimes they ask. But even when they don't, I still know that's what they're thinking. I see that look, I just up and say, 'About fifteen years is the answer to your question. And she's eight.' Some of them turn tail right away."

I was living in the city with my new girlfriend; Blythe had stayed in Tennessee. I visited every month to spend time with Dylan, staying with them for a week, an arrangement that made perfect sense to us, if not always to the girlfriends and boyfriends. In the end, though, I think Sweetheart scared away more suitors than I did, which was only one of the reasons I was astonished when Blythe told me she was getting another pig.

"Are you crazy?" I said. We were sitting on the back porch, watching Dylan splash in the pool, and looking out at a vermilion slash of sunset bleeding through the storm clouds above the roof of the old barn.

"Probably," she said.

"Explain this to me."

"I'm not sure I can."

"It's perverse."

"Look, I know it's going to be a disaster for my love life, but somehow I don't care."

The afternoon's intolerable heat was finally subsiding, the cicadas shutting down their tiny chain saws, the fireflies just waking up under logs and eaves, checking their switches. It was a moment of hiatus, of stillness between the activities of the day and the night. Sweetheart lay on her side, catching the last rays of the sun. Even Dylan seemed to pause for a moment, standing at the edge of the pool, gazing out over the pasture as it turned from pink to gray as the sun slipped beneath the treetops at the far end of the field. The air was heavy with the promise of rain. All at once I felt myself projected back in time, the light and the temperature and the scent of the air exquisitely and precisely mimetic of a previous June evening some four or five years ago, when I was a better and a happier man.

"I already paid the breeder," she said. "He's arriving at the airport tomorrow. It's a boy. Another McSwine."

"What the hell," I said. "I'll drive you."

It was no crazier, I realized, than certain aspects of my own life. And it was no longer my fight.

The next day we dropped Dylan off at preschool and then drove to the air-freight terminal. After several inquiries, we were directed to a door with plastic flaps and a gravity wheel conveyor. As we watched, three big cardboard boxes with holes punched in them parted the flaps and rolled out, GRASSMERE ZOO stamped on each one.

"What are those?" Blythe asked the men who were retrieving the boxes.

"Mice 'n' rats, I reckon," one of them said in a slow country drawl.

"Chow for the reptile house," said the other.

"I would've thought frogs," Blythe said.

"Frogs, too," said the country boy. "Frogs was last week."

As they wheeled the rodents away, a large red-and-white-striped box appeared between the flaps.

Blythe saw it before I did, and a pained expression crossed her face as she lifted her hand to her mouth. I looked again as the box emerged, sliding toward us on the steel rollers. Then I saw the blue field of stars at the other end of the box—an American flag wrapped neatly around a coffin.

"Oh my God," Blythe said.

I looked around. "Shouldn't someone . . . . be here?"

For the moment we were alone.

I looked at her. "Maybe we should . . ."

"I don't know."

"Me, neither."

At that moment a uniformed baggage handler holding a small animal carrier approached us.

"Are you the pig parents?"

Blythe nodded, gingerly taking the carrier. Tears rolled down her cheeks as she bent down to look in through the slats. "Look at him—he's so scared," she said, wiping her eyes with the back of her hand. "The poor baby."

"Maybe you should tell someone about . . . this," I said to the baggage handler, gesturing toward the coffin.

He shook his head and sighed. "Second one this week."

Back in the car, the little pig squealed like a banshee when Blythe took him out of the carrier and held him in her lap. He was about the size of a beer bottle, with black-and-white bristles, stubby legs and a straight tail that twitched incessantly. "The sweet thing," Blythe said, stroking his back. The tears reappeared as we drove down the exit ramp. "That poor boy," she said. "Why wasn't anybody there for him?"

I shook my head, not trusting my voice.

"It's so awful," she said, rubbing the piglet. "All alone, nobody to welcome him home. Oh God, my poor Jimmy."

It was, I realized, just the second time I'd heard her say her brother's name.

We drove in silence until I finally found my voice. "I'm so sorry, Blythe," I said, my voice a hoarse whisper. "I'm so goddamn sorry." It was some time before I could speak again. "Please forgive me. I never even said I was sorry."

"It's okay, McSwine," she said, turning to me and wiping my cheek. "You know my motto: 'Don't look back.'" I took her hand and lifted it to my mouth. Kissing the back of her wrist, I could smell the sweet, milky, barnyard tang of her fingers. As I squeezed her hand and pressed her fingertips to my lips, I believed there was still time and hope for me, if I could only remember always exactly how I felt at that moment.

I Love You, Honey

|

The first time it happened, Liam blamed the terrorists. He assumed that his wife, like all the other sentient residents of the city, was traumatized by the events of that September day. Deciding that this was no world into which to bring another child was a perfectly rational response, though he knew many people who'd had the exact opposite response. This, too, was understandable: affirming life in the face of so much death. He could name several children who were born nine months later, and he assumed there were hundreds, maybe thousands, more around the city—in fact, he'd read something to that effect. But Lora's was the opposite response. He didn't really begin to suspect until much later that her motives might have been more complex, less cosmic and more personal, than he had imagined.

2

Her friend LuAnne had called to say something had happened, and she'd started surfing channels with the remote in one hand and the phone in the other, seeing the same image on all the stations. She called Liam at work and his assistant said he had a meeting scheduled out of the office. Lora then tried his cell, but the call went directly to voice mail. She kept punching the redial button every few minutes. After the second plane hit, she called the office again to ask where, exactly, the meeting was, frantic with worry, trying to remember if Liam had ever mentioned any business in the World Trade Center, but now she got the assistant's recorded message. In fact, Liam's office was in TriBeCa, only seven or eight blocks from the towers, and after the first one collapsed, she could imagine any number of scenarios that might have put him in harm's way. After the second tower fell, she was convinced he was dead. And then he called, his greeting incongruously blithe.

"Hey, babe, it's me."

"Liam. Oh my God. Where *are* you?"

"At the office. Just out of a meeting. What's up?"

"Thank God," she said.

"What's wrong?"

"I thought you were dead."

"Why would I be dead?"

"Jesus, God, Liam, haven't you *heard*? Turn on the TV. Look out the window, for God's sake."

3

Liam arrived at their apartment on Waverly Place ten minutes later—less time than it would have taken him to walk from TriBeCa, but he didn't realize until later that the subway service was knocked out and that cabs had vanished from the downtown streets—so everyone later agreed—within minutes of the second plane. In fact, he'd been a few blocks away at his girlfriend's apartment on St. Mark's Place. They met there every Tuesday morning, between nine and eleven, turning off the phones, doing it exactly twice, and there had been no reason to suppose that the world would be turned upside down on this particular Tuesday. After talking to Lora, he turned on the TV, shushing Sasha as she stepped out of the bathroom, trying to figure out what the hell was happening to his city. His horror was compounded with guilt as he realized how implausible was his claim of being at the office.

"My God, I can't believe this," Sasha said, throwing her arms around him as she slumped beside him on the couch. He squirmed free and stood up. He knew it was unfair, irrational, even, but somehow he blamed her for what had happened and felt an overwhelming desire to be with his wife. Walking back across the Village, looking up warily at a looming apartment tower on Broadway, he struck on the perfect alibi.

4

Until she actually saw and touched him, Lora couldn't quite overcome her earlier conviction that he'd perished in the disaster, and he seemed just as emotional as he hugged her in the foyer, nearly crushing her ribs in his emphatic embrace. When he finally let go, she saw the tears in his eyes.

"I thought I'd never see you again."

"I was in a screening," he said. "I had no idea."
"I thought I was going to raise our baby alone."

5

The days that followed were the most vivid of his life. In retrospect, though, they sometimes seemed reduced to a set of experiences that came to seem almost clichéd by virtue of their resemblance to those of their friends, repeated endlessly over numerous cocktails: the mind-numbing hours in front of the television; the sense of disbelief; the missing friends and acquaintances; the night-mares; the acrid electrical-fire smell in the air; the spontaneous weeping, the excessive drinking. And yet they both agreed—as did everyone else—that they'd never been so conscious of the lives of others, of their own turbulent stream of consciousness, of their own mortality. And they discovered that life was never quite so precious as it was in the proximity of death. From that first night they fucked as if their survival depended on it, and with a passion neither had felt in years.

Liam was mortified at his own infidelity and brimming with the resolve to honor his marriage vows forever more. He'd felt the same resolve three weeks earlier when he learned Lora was pregnant, but somehow he hadn't managed to break it off with Sasha. He kept meaning to, but it seemed like something he had to do in person rather than over the phone or in an E-mail, and then she would greet him at her apartment door, wearing that aquamarine kimono, the mere sight of which aroused him even before she kissed him.

It was a time of lofty resolutions, of vows and renunciations. He felt incredibly lucky to have escaped this recent peccadillo unscathed, with his marriage intact, although he sometimes wondered if Lora didn't harbor suspicions, and he felt the occasional twinge of guilt about Sasha, who had no one to comfort her in this moment of collective trauma.

6

For her part, Lora was too relieved to have her husband back to inquire too deeply into his precise itinerary that day. She told herself that the clock had been reset on the morning of September 11 and that whatever happened before didn't really matter. But she couldn't help noticing that Liam seemed almost allergic to his cell phone, jumping whenever it rang over the next few days. He also seemed uncomfortable whenever the subject of people's whereabouts that morning arose, as it did constantly in the days and weeks that followed.

They were inseparable those first few days, staying in or near the apartment, clinging to each other in the aftermath, until Saturday morning, when Liam said he was going to the gym.

"Maybe I'll go with you," Lora said.

He shrugged. "If you'd like."

"No, you go ahead," she said.

She waited exactly sixty seconds and then followed him out the door and down the two flights of stairs to the double doors leading to the street, the second of which was just wafting shut. It was one of those days when the wind had shifted uptown, carrying the burned-plastic smell of smoke from Ground Zero. Her fellow pedestrians seemed skittish, the brusque, purposeful tunnel vision of the natives having been replaced by a new caution that made everyone seem like tourists. Lora didn't really have a plan, but the gym was only a few blocks away, and if she lost him on the street, she could just turn up, and if she found him there, she'd say she'd changed her mind. She watched him walking west and followed, catching sight of him at the end of the block as he turned left on Sixth—the opposite direction from the gym. She ran up Waverly and saw Liam at the next corner, waiting for the light.

He crossed the avenue, turned right and went up the steps of St. Joseph's Church, disappearing inside through the big double oak doors. She could hardly believe it. She approached stealthily and stood watching for a few minutes on the sidewalk across the street. She felt almost giddy with relief when she realized this was his secret destination. But her relief was almost immediately replaced by a sense of irritation at how cowardly it was to have lied about where he was going.

Liam had been raised as a Catholic on Long Island, and they were married in the church where he'd received his First Communion. Their wedding day was the last time she agreed to accompany him to church. The daughter of a Jewish father and an Episcopal mother, Lora had enjoyed a thoroughly secular childhood. A staunch agnostic, she used to tease him about his residual Catholicism, which she saw as a tribal habit, like his fondness for corned beef and cabbage, rather than an active belief system. She supposed it made sense that he would seek out the faith of his childhood now, in this moment of extremis. Part of her envied him this reserve source of consolation, and part of her thought he was weak for surrendering, when the going got tough, to the superstitions of his ancestors. What the hell was he doing in there anyway? It was probably a reflex, like the desire for comfort food and retro music that had swept across the city. She waited for another five minutes and then returned to the apartment, where she flipped restlessly from one news channel to another, watching the towers fall over and over again as she waited for Liam to come home.

7

Liam knelt with his head in his hands, finding the familiar darkness of the confessional, redolent of furniture polish and stale perspiration, unexpectedly comforting. When he heard the wood panel slide open, he looked up to see the silhouette of the priest behind the screen.

"Bless me, Father, for I have sinned. It's been, well, more than a year since my last confession."

"How much longer, would you say?"

"It's been . . . I think it's about four years."

"Go ahead, my son."

"I'm not sure where to begin."

8

When he returned home, Liam seemed like a different man from the twitchy neurotic who'd left the apartment a half-hour before. For the rest of the day he exhibited a maddening serenity. Lora wanted to challenge him, to crash his spiritual buzz, if that's what it was, but it seemed peevish to chide him for being in a good mood, and she couldn't think of how to engage him in an intellectual debate without acknowledging that she'd followed him. She took another Xanax, her third of the day.

"I'm thinking about going to Mass tomorrow," he said, while they waited for the check at their local bistro. "I don't know, somehow, with everything that's happened, I think it would be, you know, comforting. Of course you're welcome to join me."

"I think it's sweet," she said, pinching his cheek, "and totally understandable that you can find comfort in your old rituals, but I might feel a little hypocritical suddenly going to church just because I'm feeling emotionally needy. But that's just me. You do what you need to, honey."

That night, for the first time since Tuesday, they failed to have sex. Lora wasn't really in the mood, and was almost looking forward to letting him know she wasn't. But within moments of turning off the television set, she heard him snoring from the other pillow. Lora lay awake in the dark, feeling abandoned, thinking about the chaos outside, and the life growing within her. Though she wished she had some kind of faith, after what had happened she was hard-pressed to imagine a moral order in the universe.

9

The churches were packed that Sunday. Liam arrived fifteen minutes early for the ten o'clock Mass and even so he had to stand in the back. He felt the force of Lora's implicit admonishment, along with a kind of sociological embarrassment. Ever since he'd made his way to Stamford, he'd done all he could to distance himself from his heritage and to regard religion as an academic subject. Seeing himself now through the eyes of his friends, he felt ashamed, as if he were standing naked in a room of fully clothed adults, but at the same time he felt the exhilaration of surrender, as if he were a naked infant lying in the sun, absolved of the responsibilities of higher consciousness. For the first time since Tuesday, he felt at home and at peace in his city. He was unexpectedly moved when it came time to exchange the peace of the Lord—a folksy ritual inspired by the Second Vatican Council—which had always seemed artificial to him, the congregants stiffly shaking hands and wishing one another the peace of the Lord, but that day, he found himself clasping the hands of neighbors with special vigor and warmth, looking into their glistening eyes as he uttered, "The peace of the Lord be with you," the voices of his neighbors swelling and filling the church around him. And when the priest intoned, "Lift up your hearts," he seemed to feel his own heart swell and rise as he responded, "We have lifted them up to the Lord." And when, finally, he took the host on his tongue, letting it dissolve on the roof of his mouth, he imagined his inner being infused with light, like a cave suddenly illuminated by a torch.

After Mass he didn't feel he could return directly to the apartment. It would be like smoking a cigarette after running a marathon. He knew he couldn't face Lora in this state, any more than he'd been able to face Jenny, his last girlfriend, the teetotaler, after doing a few lines of coke. Instead, he tested this new lightness of spirit as he walked down to Canal Street, to the edge of the blue police barricades sealing off the zone of destruction from the rest of the city, and stood with his fellow citizens watching the plume of smoke that rose like a white pillar into the blue sky and tilted off to the east before diffusing into the cumulus over Brooklyn. From this distance it was an incongruously beautiful sight.

10

That night, they walked over to Norman's loft in Chelsea, where everyone was telling their stories. "I'm walking down Greenwich Street and suddenly this plane is practically on top of me," their host said, passing a joint to Jason, "this huge jet flying just above the tops of the buildings."

Jason took a hit. "Do you guys remember Carlos, the guy who used to cook for our parties?"

"The cute one with the scar above his eye?"

Jason nodded. "Missing. He was a line chef at Windows on the World."

"Jesus."

"Speaking of Jesus," Lora said, "Liam has rediscovered his faith."

"What's this?"

"He went to Mass this week." Lora walked over and ruffled his hair as if he were a child who'd just done something cute. "Didn't you, my love? I think it's sweet."

"That's great," Jason said.

"Yeah, really," Norman said. "I wish I had one to rediscover."

"Confession," Jason said. "That's what I've always envied about Catholicism. The idea that you can go into a little booth and cleanse your soul."

"I don't think I could go and tell some stranger my sins."

"Oh come on. We Jews have that, too. It's called psychoanalysis."

"But it doesn't help. I've talked to my shrink twice this week. What can he tell me? That I have every right to feel bad? That I have survivor's guilt? That I should refill my Paxil?"

Norman looked at Liam. "Did it help?"

"I suppose so," Liam said. He didn't feel he could go into it with this group. It would be like discussing sex with his parents.

Lora took his cheek in her fingers, putting her face close to his and smiling sweetly, or so it appeared, though he'd come to suspect the sincerity of this particular gesture. "We love you, honey," she said.

As soon as he could, he retreated to a neutral distance; at that moment his phone rang and he answered it, happy for the interruption.

"Liam, it's me," Sasha said. "Don't hang up. I'm so miserable. I need to see you."

He shouldn't have looked to see if Lora was watching him, because she was. "I'm sorry, but you've got the wrong number," he said, feeling the heat in his cheeks. He turned off the ringer before slipping the phone back in his pocket.

"The phones are still completely screwed up," Jason said.

||

"So you've become a believer?" she asked, smiling brightly. It was the second Sunday of the new era and he'd just asked her if she wanted to join him at Mass. He shrugged. "I just . . . at this particular moment in time, I'm feeling a sense of, I don't know, spiritual yearning. Is that so surprising, really?"

"If that's what you need, then I think you should by all means go to Mass."

"Look, I know you feel differently, but I don't want to argue about this."

"Who's arguing?" She reached over and stroked his cheek, pinching it between her thumb and forefinger. "I love you."

"Maybe I'm weak, maybe I'm being hypocritical, but just indulge me in this, okay? If you don't want to go, I'll understand."

Lora assumed Liam's recrudescence of faith would fade along with the initial shock of that terrifying day. She was kind of assuming the same thing about her own Xanax consumption; she'd cut back again once things returned to normal, but right now it seemed impossible to get through the day without forty or fifty milligrams.

After Liam left, she turned on the TV again, another escalating addiction that would surely subside in the weeks to come. She was watching the Taliban spokesman, defiant in his black beard and black robes, when she heard Liam's phone vibrating on the coffee table. She noticed that he'd turned off the ringer days ago, but now it was buzzing like a big flat beetle on the glass. She picked it up. "Hello?"

There was silence on the other end.

"Did he tell you I'm pregnant?" Lora said, then snapped the phone shut and went to the bathroom and took two more Xanax.

For some reason, she remembered the conversation at Norman's loft. She'd almost forgotten about the whole confession thing, but suddenly she wondered if that had been the point of Liam's new faith: to clear his soul of mortal sin before the next plane hit.

12

Liam's office was inside the restricted zone south of Canal, and for the first week or so he didn't even think about going to work, but then a friend invited him to use his space in Chelsea. He went back to work the second Monday, not that he foresaw a big demand anytime soon for the kind of edgy independent films he produced. When he got home that night, he could tell that something was wrong. His first thought, on seeing her stony expression, was that somehow she'd learned about Sasha.

"Any thoughts about dinner?" he asked.

"I'm not hungry."

"Shall I cook something?"

"I told you; I'm not hungry."

"I brought some DVDs from the office. *Hedwig and the Angry Inch* and *Riding in Cars with Boys.*"

"I don't think so," she said. Tears were pooling in her eyes, though she looked more angry than sad.

"What's wrong?"

"The baby's gone," she said.

"Gone?"

The tears were coursing down her cheeks, but her manner was defiant. When he tried to embrace her, she pushed him away and said, "I ended it."

13

Eventually, in his mind, it seemed, the abortion became subsumed into the narrative of the collective trauma. Liam went out and got drunk that night, but in the succeeding days he seemed unwilling to confront her about her motives, as if he were afraid their marriage couldn't survive the revelation of certain facts. At some point, after telling her that he believed in the sanctity of life from the moment of conception, he made the decision to forgive her, just as she, in turn, forgave him, though neither of them ever acknowledged his transgression. But he had presumably confessed his sin, and she sometimes wondered how he squared his own faith with her action, and her own unshriven state. Apparently, in his mind, she had committed murder. But divorce, too, was a mortal sin. As much as she despised his faith, she kind of liked the idea that Catholicism protected her matrimonial monopoly.

Most of the noble resolutions of that period gradually faded away, but Liam continued to attend Mass, without making a big deal of it. The fact that he stopped talking about it had convinced her of his seriousness. For her part, she tried not to give him a hard time.

The following spring, Lora was pregnant again. The days between the morning the stick on the home pregnancy test turned blue and the evening their son was delivered in December were among the happiest of their marriage. After a long period of apartment hunting and soul-searching—both of them of an age to have used the phrase "bridge and tunnel" to denote those living in the hinterlands—they bought a town house in Brooklyn's Boerum Hill. Like most converts, they became strident proselytizers, declaiming the virtues of the restaurants on Smith Street and insisting that it was only ten minutes by subway to the Village. They loved telling not only their friends but also each other how much they didn't miss Manhattan, though eventually this became something of a moot point when Liam started spending half his time in Los Angeles after one of his scripts was picked up by HBO shortly after Jeremy's second birthday. Lora couldn't pretend that it wasn't hard on her, being left behind to take care of the baby. And she couldn't help wondering what he was doing when he wasn't working, despite his declarations that every waking moment was consumed by the show. But he was an attentive father and lover during his sojourns in Brooklyn, and one morning she woke him at his hotel in Los Angeles to tell him that she was pregnant.

"That's fantastic," he said.

"You're happy?"

"I couldn't be happier. Aren't you?"

"I don't know. I'd be happier if you were here right now."

"I'll be home the day after tomorrow. We'll celebrate."

Unpacking his suitcase two mornings later while he slept in, she found, mixed in with his shirts, a baby-blue silk teddy trimmed with black lace.

14

When Liam woke up that morning, he was alone. Sitting up in bed, he saw his suitcase, propped open on the floor, and recognized the light-blue undergarment on top as belonging to his production assistant. For years he'd behaved himself and remained faithful to Lora, but recently he and Lanie had been working late, and one night she'd kissed him and he'd been unable to resist. He'd gone to confession the next afternoon, but it had happened again several times since. He didn't know how her nightie had gotten into his suitcase, but the more troubling question was why it was so flagrantly displayed, when he was ninety percent certain he hadn't opened the bag when he came in the previous night. What the hell was he supposed to do now? He finally decided to bury it beneath his shirts and hope that it never surfaced again.

He descended the stairs with trepidation, but he couldn't read anything unusual in Lora's demeanor when he found her in the kitchen with Jeremy in her arms, attached to her breast. That she was still breast-feeding Jeremy at two and a half was a point of contention, but he wasn't about to get into it now. Lora seemed delighted to see him. "Here's Daddy," she said. "And we love Daddy, don't we? Yes, we do." She shuffled across the floor in her slippers, clutching Jeremy to her chest, and took Liam's left cheek in her fingers, pinching and pulling his face close to hers. "We love you so much, Daddy."

All weekend he waited for the accusation, but it never came. After two days at home, he would almost have welcomed a confrontation, but Lora seemed to have finely calibrated her chilliness to a degree or two above the freezing point, and when they had another couple over for dinner on Saturday, she was overly effusive, gratuitously declaring her love on several occasions. Before the Robertsons arrived, he'd suggested they tell them about the pregnancy, feeling that the announcement would make it more real, might lodge the fetus more firmly in Lora's uterine wall, but Lora said it was way too early for that.

While Liam was mixing the margaritas, Lora told her new joke: "What's the biggest drawback to being an atheist? Give up? No one to talk to during orgasm."

Shortly after she put dessert on the table, she stabbed him with a fork. She was talking to Donna about private schools when suddenly she brought her clenched fist, clutching her fork, down on his thigh, impaling him through his jeans.

If Liam, in his surprise, had been able to suppress a shriek of pain, it's possible the attack would have passed unnoticed. As it was, Lora made the whole thing seem like an unfortunate accident, an absentminded gesture.

"Oh my God. Oh, Liam honey. You know how I'm always grabbing your thigh. It's like, shit, I forgot I had a goddamn fork in my hand. Poor baby, you're bleeding. I'm so sorry." She showered him with apologies and first aid, and even after the Robertsons had left, she maintained an air of concern and contrition. For his part, Liam was too frightened to confront her. He only hoped that she'd gotten it all out of her system at once. Maybe now they could go on as if nothing had happened.

Back in L.A., he told Lanie that it was over between them, citing the pregnancy, and she seemed to understand. In retrospect, he found it remarkable that communication between a man and woman with a sexual history could be so straightforward.

A few nights later, they were crashing a script, four of them working in the office till midnight, when they decided to move to his hotel suite, where they could order up a room-service supper. Liam was in the bathroom when the phone rang, and he rushed out in a panic. He knew who was calling.

Lanie was still holding the receiver. "Hello?"

He grabbed the phone away from her and heard only the dial tone. It was three-ten in the morning; it wasn't hard to guess what Lora, if it had been Lora, was thinking. There was no way of verifying the incoming number on the hotel phone.

"What's the matter?" Brodie asked.

He dialed his home number in Brooklyn. After a half-dozen rings, he heard his own voice explaining that no one could come to the phone right now. "Honey, it's Liam. Listen, I thought you might have called just now and I wanted to make sure everything's okay out there. We're all here just finishing up on the script for tomorrow, me and Brodie and Issac and Lanie. I guess you're asleep. Just wanted to make sure everything was okay. Big kiss."

He called throughout the day, but Lora never answered. When he still couldn't reach her the following afternoon, he told his colleagues he had an emergency and caught the red-eye to New York.

15

She was in bed with Jeremy when he came in at seven. She said she wasn't feeling well, that she had cramps and was bleeding.

"Are you all right?" he said breathlessly.

"Not really," she said.

"The baby?"

"There is no baby."

"You had a miscarriage?"

"No." She shook her head. "Not a miscarriage."

Having arrived all tense and alert, he seemed to deflate before her eyes, slumping to the foot of the bed. "How could you do this?"

"It's just a procedure," she said. Of course, she knew it was more than that to him. To him, it was a mortal sin.

"It's a life," he said. "Is this what happened the last time, too? You were punishing me?"

"Punishing you for what, my love?" Despite the pain, she managed a bright smile. "I just wasn't ready for another child. I didn't think we were ready."

"But you know how I feel about this," he said. "How am I supposed to live with you after this?"

"Of course you'll live with me. With us—your wife and son. What else would you do? You know I love you, honey."

The Madonna of Turkey Season

It came to seem like our own special Thanksgiving tradition—one of us inevitably behaving very badly. The role was passed around the table from year to year like some kind of ceremonial torch, or a seasonal virus: the weeping and gnashing of teeth, the breaking of glass, the hurling of accusations, the final nosedive into the mashed potatoes or the shag carpet. Sometimes it even fell to our guests—friends, girlfriends, wives—the disease apparently communicable. We were three boys who'd lost their mother—four if you counted Dad, five if you counted Brian's best friend, Foster Creel, who'd lost his own mother about the same time we did and always spent Thanksgiving with us—and for many years there had been no one to tell us not to pour that pivotal seventh drink, not to chew with our mouths open, not to say *fuck* at the dinner table.

We kept bringing other women to the table to try to fill the hole, but they were never able to impose peace for long. Sometimes they were catalysts, and occasionally they even initiated the hostilities—perhaps their way of trying to fit in. Our father never brought another woman to the table, though many tried to invite themselves, and our young girlfriends remarked on how handsome he was and what a waste it was. "I had my great love, and how could I settle for anything less," he'd say as he poured himself another Smirnoff and the neighbor widows and divorcées dashed themselves against the windowpanes like birds.

Sometimes, although not always, the mayhem boiled up again at Christmas, in the sacramental presence of yet another turkey carcass, with a new brother or guest in the role of incendiary device, though memories of the most recent Thanksgiving were often enough to spare us the spectacle for another eleven months. I suppose we all had a lot to be thankful for, socioeconomically speaking, but for some reason we chose to dwell instead on our grievances. *How come you went to Finlay's high school play and not mine? How could you have fucked Karen Watley when you knew I was in love with her?*

We would arrive Tuesday night from prep school or college, or on Wednesday night from New York, where we were working at a bank while writing a play, or from Vermont, where we were building a log cabin with our roommate from Middlebury before heading up to Stowe at first snow for a season of ski bumming. Dad would take the latter part of the week off, until he retired, which was when things really became dangerous. The riotous foliage that briefly enflamed the chaste New England hills was long gone, leaving the monochromatic landscape of winter: the gray stone walls of the early settlers, the silver trunks of the maples, the white columns of birch.

Manly hugs were exchanged at the kitchen door. Cocktails were offered and accepted. Girlfriends and roommates were introduced. The year of the big snow, footwear was scraped on the blade of the cast-iron boot cleaner outside the door. Dad was particularly pleased with this implement, and always pointed it out to guests, not because he was particularly fastidious about mud and snow, but because it seemed to signify all the supposed charm and tradition of old New England (as opposed to, say, its intolerance of immigrants and its burning of young girls at the stake), although he'd bought this particular boot scraper once upon a time at the local True Value hardware store. But somehow Dad had convinced himself that it had been planted here by the early settlers of the Massachusetts Bay Colony, in between skirmishes with the Iroquois and the Mohicans. He liked to think of himself as an old Yankee, despite the fact that when his grandfathers arrived in Boston, the windows were full of NO IRISH NEED APPLY signs and they weren't likely to be invited to scrape their boots at anybody's front door. A century and a half later, though, we lived in a big white house with green shutters, which Dad inevitably described as "Colonial," though it was built in the 1920s to resemble something a hundred years older.

Most of the girls we brought—a cavalcade of blondes— were judged by their resemblance to our mother, except when it seemed, as was the case a couple of times with Brian, they'd been deliberately chosen for their contro- versial darkness. Each of us could see how his brother's girlfriend was a pale imitation of Mom and our own were one-offs who shared some of her best qualities. The girls, for their part, must have been a little daunted at first to discover the patterns of traits they'd cherished as unique.

As different as we were, we were all recognizably alike, with the same unruly hair, the same heavy-browed, smiley eyes and all our invisible resemblances, born and bred. Brian, the eldest, kept things lively by bringing a different girl every year; we called him "the Kennedy of the family." The rest of us took after Dad, who liked to say that Mom was his only true love. Mike had been with Jennifer since his freshman year at Colby, and Aidan met his future wife, Alana, before he was twenty. Actually, Brian showed up two years in a row with Janis, whom he eventually married, much to our and then his own chagrin. The second time, she threw the entire uncarved turkey at Brian's head, a scene that eventually showed up in his second play. Another year, he and Foster nearly came to blows at the table when it came out that they'd lately been sleeping with the same girl. It took two of us to restrain Brian.

Brian's personal life, with all its chaos, *Sturm und Drang*, was the workshop version of his professional life, a laboratory for drama. And of course he wrote about us. Mike said at the time that the phrase "thinly disguised" was too chubby by half to describe Brian's relation to his source material. His first play revolved around the death of a mother from cancer. There seemed to be a number of those that particular season, but his was the most success-ful. We all went down to the opening night at the New York Theatre Workshop. The play was directed by Foster, who'd been his best friend ever since Choate, and had gone with him to Yale Drama. We sat there, stunned in the aftermath, as the applause thundered around us. It was hard to know how to react. In the play, Brian seemed to be making a special claim for himself with regard to our mother, in that the character who was obviously him had been more loved and more devastated than the others.

Then there was the question of his portrayal of the rest of us. On the one hand, as brothers we wanted to say, *Hey, that's not me,* and on the other, *But wait a minute; that is me.* He'd put us in an untenable position. Brian was a great sophist, and if you complained about the parallels between his life and art, he would start declaiming about the autobiographical basis of *Long Day's Journey into Night* or point out that "your" character had gone to Deerfield, when you'd actually gone to Hotchkiss. And if you complained about inaccuracies—denied that you'd ever, for example, had carnal relations with the family dog—he would cite poetic license or remind you that you'd been banging on a moment before about resemblances and that this clearly demonstrated the fictionality of his master-piece.

At first, it was hard to tell how Dad felt about it. He put on a brave face and went over to Phoebe's, the bar down the block, to celebrate with Brian and the cast. He seemed to be in shock. But later, in the cab back to the hotel, and in the bar there, he kept asking us, over and over again, some variant of the question, "Was I such a bad father?" In truth, he didn't come off all that badly, but we all had a hard time not viewing the play as a flawed family memoir. He also cornered Foster, our unofficial fourth brother, whom for years Dad had consulted as a kind of emotional translator in his efforts to understand Brian.

"Every artist interprets the world through the prism of his own narcissism," Foster told him that night. "He doesn't think you're a bad father. He forgot about you the day he started writing the play. All the characters in the play, even the ones who look and sound like you, are Brian, or else they're foils for Brian." I don't think my father knew whether to be reassured or worried by this. Of course, he'd long known Brian was massively self-absorbed, prone to exaggeration and outright mendacity. But he seemed pleased with the judgment, repeated to us all many times later, that Brian was an artist. At last, he seemed to feel, there was an explanation for his temperament, and his deviations from what my father considered proper behavior: the drugs, the senseless prevarications, the childhood interest in poetry. For Dad, Foster's assessment counted as much as subsequent accolades in the *Times* and elsewhere.

That year, Brian brought Cassie Haynes, the actress, who played his former girlfriend Rita Cosovich in the play, although of course he denied that the character was based on Rita, and we all wondered if Rita would, on balance, be more offended by the substance of her portrait or flattered by its appearance, Cassie being a babe of the first order. She caused a bit of a sensation around the neighborhood that Thanksgiving, husbands coming from three streets down to ask after the leaf blower they thought they might possibly have lent to Dad earlier in the fall. When we heard she was coming, we all thought, Great, just what we need, a prima donna actress, though we couldn't help liking her, and hoping she would come back during bathing-suit season.

Brian's play gave us something to fight about at the Thanksgiving board for years to come, beginning that first

November after the opening, when the wounds were still
fresh. Mike, the middle brother, was the first to take up
the cause after the cocktail hour had been prolonged due
to some miscalculation about the turkey. Mike's fiancée,
Jennifer, had volunteered to cook the bird that year, and
while she would later become our chief and favorite cook,
this was her first attempt at a turkey, and rather than
relying on Mom's old copy of *The Fannie Farmer Cook-
book,* she'd insisted on adapting a chicken recipe from
Julia Child's *Mastering the Art of French Cooking.* When
Dad attempted to carve the turkey the first time, the legs
were still pink and raw and the bird was slammed back in
the oven, giving us all another jolly hour and a half to
deplete the bar. We might have given Jennifer less grief if
she hadn't initially tried to defend herself, insisting that
the French preferred their birds rare and implying that a
thoroughly cooked bird was unsophisticated. When we
finally sat down to eat, Brian said grace without letting her
off the hook: "*Notre père, qui aime la volaille crue, que ton
nom soit sanctifié* . . .*"

Mike interrupted, him, asking how he'd like a well-
done drumstick up the ass. Dad demanded a truce, and for
several minutes peace prevailed, until Dad started to talk
about Mom in that maudlin way of his, a recitation that
always relied heavily on the concept of her sainthood.
Usually we all collaborated in changing the subject and
leading him out of this quagmire of grieving nostalgia, but
now Mike wanted to open the subject for debate.

"She didn't deserve to suffer," Dad was saying.

"Apparently, the person who suffered the most was
Brian," Mike said. "At least that's the impression I got

from the play. I mean, sure, Mom was dying of cancer and all, but I never realized it hurt Brian so much to administer her shots the one night that he actually managed to sit up with her. Maybe I'm a philistine, but it seemed to me like the point was the one who really suffered wasn't Mom, it was Brian."

"Okay, okay," Brian said. "I'm sorry I said grace in French."

"That's not really the point," Mike said.

"Oh, but I think it is."

"I don't blame you for trying to change the subject, you self-centered prick. But you know what? We all grew up in the same house. And we all saw the play."

"Now, boys," Dad said.

"You, of all people, know what I'm talking about," Mike said, pointing a fork at our father. "Let's be honest. You were freaked-out by the play."

Dad didn't want to go down this road. "I had a few . . . concerns."

"Don't pussy out, Dad. We've talked about this, for Christ's sake. Why are we all so worried about Brian's feelings? It's not like he lost any sleep worrying about ours."

"Actually," Cassie said, "I happen to know he was very worried about your feelings. I think Foster will agree with me."

"It's not like he shows it," Mike said.

"I think it's wonderful how women attribute lofty ideals and fine feelings to us," Foster said. "But, I'm sorry, if Brian had spent much time worrying about your feelings, it wouldn't have been much of a fucking play."

This quip might have defused the situation, but Mike, like a giant freighter loaded with grievances, was unable to change course. Brian parried his continuing assault with glib little irrelevancies until Mike eventually stormed out of the room, spilling red wine all over the Irish linen tablecloth, but the rest of us considered ourselves fortunate that it wasn't blood. Mike had the fiercest temper in the family, and he was three inches taller and thirty pounds heavier than his elder brother.

The whole exchange was pretty representative. While Brian had always charmed and finessed and fibbed his way through life, Mike had a fierce stubborn honesty and a big hardwood chip on his shoulder, which was in some measure a reflection of his belief that Brian had already claimed the upper bunk bed of life before he came along and had a chance to choose for himself. If Brian were assailing a castle, he would try to sneak in the back door by seducing the scullery maid; Mike would butt his head against the portcullis until it or he gave way. Mike's youthful transgressions weren't necessarily more numerous or egregious, but, unlike Brian, he was inevitably caught and held accountable, in part because he considered it dishonest to hide them. Brian never let the facts compromise his objective, and he seemed almost allergic to them. When he got caught with marijuana, he had an elaborate, if hackneyed, story about how he was holding it for a friend. But when Mike decided to grow it, he did so out in the open, planting rows between the corn and tomatoes in the vegetable garden, until someone finally told our mother, who'd been giving tours of the garden, the true identity of the mystery herb. Back then, none of us could have predicted that Mike would eventually be the one to follow our father to business school and General Electric, that he'd be diplomatic enough to negotiate the hazards of corporate culture. His reformation owed a lot to Jennifer, starting that first year at Colby. It took us a long time to learn to love her—my father was furious over her sophomore art-class critique of our parish church—but there was no denying her anodyne effect on Mike.

The year before Mike nearly throttled Brian, it was Aidan's turn. He was the baby of the family, which seemed to be his complaint—that we treated him as such. That we didn't give him enough respect. The specific catalyst, this Thanksgiving, was obscure. That he was drunk in the manner unique to inexperienced drinkers— he was a senior at Hotchkiss at the time—didn't especially help his case, and sensing this, he became even more frustrated and strident.

"Just because I'm younger . . . it doesn't give you guys the right to treat me like I'm a *kid*. Mom wouldn't have let you. If she was here, she'd tell you."

"If she were here," Brian said.

"That's *exactly* what I mean. Treating me like a friggin' baby."

We all found it cute that even in his cups, Aidan had used the euphemism rather than the Anglo-Saxonism itself. He wasn't yet ready to cuss in front of Dad. Brian and Mike started sniggering, which further infuriated Aidan, who pounded his fist down on his plate, breaking it in half and cutting his hand on his steak knife, which had been freshly sharpened by Dad that morning. We all

agreed that Jennifer was the only one sober enough to
drive to the emergency room.

The touch-football games preceding dinner were sometimes an outlet for aggression that might otherwise have
overflowed at the table, but it occasionally spilled over, as
when Brian accused Mike of unnecessary roughness on the
field that afternoon. At Christmas, the sport was hockey,
assuming that the pond was sufficiently frozen. Our
mother, who believed that exercise and fresh air were
essential ingredients of the good life, had inaugurated both
of these activities.

We really should have just canceled Thanksgiving the
year the movie came out. Anyone could have predicted
disaster. Brian spent more than three years working on the
screenplay, on his own at first and eventually in collaboration with the director. (His second play, about preppy
young bohemians in TriBeCa, had opened to mixed
reviews and closed after an eight-week run.) Somewhere
in the screenwriting process, the story had acquired a new
complication, when the dying mother confides in her
sensitive son about her affair with his father's best friend.

In fact, Dad's best friend lived in San Francisco, as
Brian was quick to point out later, but still, it made us
wonder. Mom had been popular with most of the men in
our parents' circle of friends, and one husband, Tom
Fleishman, had always seemed almost comically smitten.
Now we started to question if it was really a joke, the way
Fleischman had always mooned around Mom, or whether
Brian had really been the recipient of some deathbed
confession. Everyone in town had the same question,
including Katy Fleishman, who called Dad in a fury after

seeing the movie in September, demanding to know what he knew, and it soon became the talk of the country club. The play had been a distant rumor, but the movie was right there next door to the Pathmark store, in the Regal Cinema multiplex, which had replaced the old downtown theaters where we'd watched *Jaws* and *Summer of '42*. And it was more successful than some might have hoped, buoyed by the performance of Maureen Firth as the wife and mother. The movie played at the Regal for seven weeks. Everyone we knew went to see it.

Brian had warned us, to some extent. On the one hand, he assured us, his vision hadn't been compromised. On the other hand, accommodations had been made, nuances flattened, whispers amplified, subtexts excavated with a backhoe and laid bare. In the play there was a rumor of infatuation.

None of us, Foster excepted, had been invited to the premiere in L.A., or rather, we'd all received a phone call from Brian, who had mentioned in passing "a big industry ratfuck" and said: "I'm not even sure I'm going myself."

And none of us knew quite what to say after we'd seen it. Brian wrote Dad a letter, assuring him that the alleged affair was strictly a Hollywood plot device and had nothing to do with reality. Dad called Foster in New York and was repeatedly reassured. Mike called Brian, threatening to kick his ass, and while the conversation was hardly conclusive, Brian swore that the affair was just a sensationalistic fiction, and it seemed as if maybe we had all had our say by the time Thanksgiving had come around. We were hoping against hope that the issue would just go away; in an unprecedented move, we even decided to water down the vodka just to keep Dad from getting too maudlin.

And for the first time since any of us could remember, it looked as if we might pass a relatively peaceful Thanksgiving, having made it all the way to the pumpkin pie without major fireworks. But despite the watered vodka, we could see Dad's eyes glazing over with melancholy reminiscence.

"I must have let her down somehow," he said during a lull in the discussion of the Patriots' season.

All of us were smart enough to pretend we hadn't heard this remark, but Aidan's fiancée was still new to the family.

"Let whom down, Mr. C.?"

"Carolyn. I must've let her down. She must have needed something I couldn't give her."

"But why would you think that?" Jennifer asked.

"Oh, for Christ's sake," Mike said, throwing his napkin down on the table. "Look at what you've done, Brian. Now he actually believes it."

"Dad," Brian said, "I told you! It never happened. It's fiction."

"It's slander," Mike said. "I still can't understand why the hell you'd drag our mother's name into the gutter like that."

"It's not our mother. It's not her name. It's a character in a movie."

"A character based on our mother."

"I just must have failed her," Dad said, oblivious to the conversation around him.

"Dad, listen to me. It never happened. I'm sorry. It's my fault. I shouldn't have written what I wrote. It was the director's idea, a cheap plot device. It isn't true."

"I always thought it was harmless," Dad said. "They used to talk at parties, and I knew they had things in common. Your mother had so many interests, art and theater, and I couldn't really talk to her about those things. I knew she and Tom talked. But I thought that's all it was."

"That *is* all it was," Brian said. "At least so far as I know."

"I know she told you things," he said to Brian. "Things she couldn't tell me."

"Not that, Dad. She never told me anything like that."

"After my operation," he said, "I was afraid. I was afraid of physical, you know, exertion."

"Dad, that's enough."

"Are you happy with yourself?" Mike asked as the tears rolled down our father's cheeks.

"Well, who's for a smoke outside?" Foster said, rising from the table. Although Dad was a lifelong smoker, our mother had, toward the end of her life, insisted that all smoking be done outdoors, a rule that Dad himself continued to observe and enforce after she was gone.

A half-hour after we put Dad to bed, Mike tackled Brian and got him in a headlock, choking him and rubbing his face in the snow. "Tell the truth, goddamn it. What did she tell you? Is it true?"

"I told you: It's not true. She never told me anything."

But nothing could ever quite dispel the doubt for us. Dad might have been forgiven for lying low, but he was determined to show himself on the local holiday party circuit. A week before Christmas, after three cocktail parties, he crashed his Mustang into an elm tree half a mile from the house.

Mike, who was working in Schenectady, was the first to arrive at the hospital. Dad was in intensive care. Aidan drove over from Amherst, arriving shortly before midnight. Brian and Foster arrived from New York just as the sun was rising and Dad was declared stable. We all spent the day at the hospital and that night traded shifts in the waiting room. Dad looked gruesome when we finally got to see him, his face bruised and puffy and green where it wasn't bandaged, his leg in traction. He was pretty doped up. "Don't tell your mother," he said when he saw us. "I don't want her to worry."

The doctor, who'd tended our mother in her final days, said, "It's the Demerol."

"We could all use some of that," Foster said.

We moved between the hospital and the house for the next ten days, keeping ourselves busy with Christmas preparations. We found a perfectly shaped blue spruce tree in the woods at the edge of the lake and we retrieved the ornaments from the attic in the old boxes from England's department store, closed years before, with Mom's block letters fading on the cardboard: CHRISTMAS LIGHTS, CHRISTMAS ANGELS, CHRISTMAS BULBS. We avoided talking about what had happened or why, concentrating instead on the practical details.

The lake had frozen early that year. After lunch on Christmas Eve, we gathered up our gear, called Ricky and Ted Quinlan next door, and trudged down for the annual hockey game. It was Foster, Ted and Aidan against Brian,

Ricky and Mike. Brian's team scored two quick goals. Aidan, who had the fiercest competitive streak of any of us, started to get physical. First he hooked Brian's skate and tripped him; then he body-checked him into the rocks of the causeway. Brian returned the favor the next time he came down the ice with the puck, knocking Aidan off into the bulrushes. He came out swinging, and caught Brian in the helmet with his stick. Then he threw him down and knelt on top of him, ripping of his helmet and punching his face. By the time we pulled him off, there was blood everywhere and one of Brian's teeth was protruding through his lip.

"You bastard," Aidan sobbed. "You selfish bastard."

Brian turned away and limped up the hill, leaving a trail of blood on the ice.

When we got back up to the house, Brian was gone.

Dad came home on New Year's Day. Aidan took winter term off from school to be with him, and Mike came over from Schenectady on the weekends. Brian called from New York to check in. Neither the fight on the ice nor his sudden departure was ever discussed again. From time to time, in his cups, Dad would ask Brian about our mother, and he would always insist that both the affair and the confession were completely fictional. Dad once confronted Tom Fleishman at the country club and he, too, denied it. But Dad could never put the question out of his mind, any more than he could walk without a cane.

Mike and Jennifer had three boys, and he became the youngest vice-president ever at GE. Aidan spent a year with the U.S. ski team before marrying Alana and going back to Hotchkiss to teach. Foster, one of the most respected directors in New York, recently married Cassie Haynes, the actress who first appeared at our house as Brian's date. We go down to see his plays from time to time.

Brian moved to Los Angeles a few weeks after Aidan busted his lip. He wrote a TV pilot, and while that project died, it led to a job as a staff writer for a long-running comedy show. We can't help feeling relieved that he's not writing about the family, and Dad watches the show every week. Brian is very well paid for his efforts and has been dating a series of extremely pretty actresses. But it also feels somehow like a cheat, a big fucking letdown. After all these years of having to put up with the idea of Brian as a great genius, of knowing that our mother believed in his special destiny, we feel like the least he could do would be to justify her favor and her hopes, instead of spending his days writing mother-in-law jokes. Nothing short of greatness could justify the doubt he cast on her memory. Foster believes that he's doing penance and that he'll go back to his real work someday.

In the meantime, we haven't all been together at Thanksgiving since Dad's accident. Now, when the leaves turn red and yellow and the grass turns white with morning frost, we feel the loss all over again. It's like we were a goddess cult that gathered once a year and now our faith has wavered. It's not that we couldn't forgive her anything. But our simple certainties have been shaken. Although we will always be Catholics, we long ago gave up on the Father, the Son and the Holy Ghost. We were a coven of Mariolatry, devoted to the Virgin. Brian believed in art, but lately he seems to have lost the faith. We find it hard to believe in anything we can't see or explain according to the immutable laws imbued in science class. We always believed in you, Mother, more than anything, but we never for a moment thought you were human.

Everything Is Lost

Sabrina decided to throw Kyle a surprise party for his thirty-fifth. Her biggest concern was that she wouldn't be able to keep it a secret—so pleased was she with the whole idea. She liked to say she shared all her thoughts and feelings with Kyle. "I tell him everything," she would say. And Kyle would say the same.

She'd been talking to the owner of the Golden Bowl—the hottest new place in TriBeCa—telling him she expected maybe forty or fifty people for the party, dropping some names in hopes of getting him down a little on the price, when Kyle walked into the bedroom and threw himself across the duvet.

"Who was that?" he asked, stroking her knee after she quickly hung up.

"Just a fact checker."

Much to her relief, he didn't seem to notice she was blushing; at least she assumed the heat in her cheeks had to be visible. She felt so transparent that she could hardly believe he didn't sense something amiss.

She suddenly realized that her preparations would be complicated by the fact that the bedroom walls stopped six feet short of the ceiling in their loft. She didn't usually think about it, except when Kyle was being particularly loud on the phone in the other room or the time her brother had spent the night on their sofa and she'd been self-conscious about having sex. When they'd first seen the loft and the Realtor had suggested the walls could be extended up to the ceiling, Sabrina had remarked, rather smugly, that they didn't need privacy. Walls were for people who weren't really in love.

"What was that you were saying about Toby Clench?" he asked.

"Toby Clench?" She was trying to buy a minute to think of what to say.

"I thought I heard you mention his name."

"He collects Brancott's work."

"Who's Brancott?"

"The artist I'm writing about."

"Oh, right. God, I can't believe that son of a bitch is collecting art," he said, again not noticing that she was blushing. He was stroking her knee, moving in the direction of her thigh, pursuing his own secret agenda. If she hadn't been so flustered, she would already have realized he'd come into the bedroom in search of nooky. She could have two jugglers and three elephants in the room and he wouldn't notice when he was in this particular state of anticipation. It was so simple—sweet, really. All she needed to do was administer a quick blow job. Sometimes it was so much easier than the full production. And she'd never heard him complain.

She reached down, unbuttoned his jeans, and slipped her hands inside his boxers. He moaned and lay back on the duvet. Spontaneous sex—one of the perks of the freelance life.

Sabrina worked at a desk in the bedroom. Kyle taught writing at N.Y.U. and had an office there. On Tuesdays and Thursdays he had classes and office hours, but most other days he liked to work at home at the kitchen table. Sabrina had been his student a couple years ago and now was writing articles to help pay the bills while intermittently working on her first novel. She loved that they shared a sacred vocation—literature, he liked to say, was their religion—and one that allowed them to spend so much time together.

When she was working, she'd hear him pacing around on the uneven old wooden floors. Sometimes she could hear him humming, or even singing, when concentrating deeply, and she loved the idea that he was working on some short story that might appear in *The Paris Review* or *The New Yorker*. And while he must have been able to hear her on the phone, he didn't seem to mind. They'd check up on each other, intermittently, in one room or the other, and if she didn't hear him for a few minutes, she would go out to find out what he was doing. Sometimes, irrationally, she was afraid that he wouldn't be there. He often came into the bedroom with that earnest, hungry look on his face, and if she wasn't too busy, they'd fall into bed and devour each other. This routine had seemed wonderful until she needed a little privacy. Was it her imagination, or was he more housebound than usual this week? She kept waiting for him to leave so she could make her calls.

Though she knew it wasn't fair, she grew increasingly irritated as he failed to do so.

"How do people who live in lofts have affairs?" she asked her friends one night over drinks at the Odeon.

"They have offices," Daisy said.

Kyle's office, she recalled, was the first place they'd ever had sex.

The next day she told Kyle she had to go out to conduct an interview, hoping she sounded casual enough to be convincing. He was sprawled on the sofa, reading a manuscript. "Have fun," he said.

In the elevator she wondered, somewhat peevishly, if he ever even thought about her whereabouts. She could be on her way to some assignation, though in fact she was going to check out the restaurant for his party.

The owner, Brom Kendall, had offered to show her around. She recognized him from his picture in *New York* magazine, where he'd been included in a feature on hot restaurateurs. He was wearing a black leather jacket over a white T-shirt, and his cleft chin and a slightly crooked nose just barely saved him from being too handsome. For some reason, she felt awkward. She had a notion that he would be conceited, although in fact he seemed a little shy as he shook her hand.

"How about a drink," he said after they'd completed their short tour of the restaurant, which, in broad daylight, without its glittering clientele, seemed to her interchangeable with a dozen others in the neighborhood. Kind of an Armani palate: taupe walls, Black Wood trim, gray leather upholstery and moody vintage black-and-white photos of scantily clad women.

Not wanting to seem unfriendly or uptight, she said she'd have a Ketel One and tonic. He went behind the bar to mix the drinks while she took a seat on the other side.

He told her that for years he'd been an actor but that then one day he'd realized it was never going to happen. Besides, he liked people; he liked food . . .

It wasn't a terribly original story—she was glad she didn't have to write it—but his obvious sincerity made it interesting. She was expecting him to be glib. "Sometimes that's what I think about my writing," she said, "like I should give it up for something practical."

"I thought that piece you did for *Black Book* was really insightful," he said, surprising her. "The one about the new chick lit."

"Wow, I'm, like, amazed." So much so that she was suddenly talking like a moron. It didn't occur to her until later that he'd probably Googled her the night before, after she first called. Still, it felt good, knowing that someone besides friends and family had read it.

He asked how she'd gotten into writing, which led her to explain that Kyle had been her writing teacher.

"Huh. How long have you two been together?"

"A little over a year."

"It's very cool of you to throw a party for him. I'd be so blown away if someone did that for me."

"Nobody's ever thrown a surprise party for you? You don't seem like the kind of guy who's been totally deprived of female attention."

"Not the *right* anybody," he said, looking at her with an intensity that made the remark seem significant.

Once again she found herself blushing. "I guess I should be getting back," she said, swilling the rest of her drink and rising to her feet.

"If you have any questions, just call," he said, handing her a card.

Kyle went to his office on Monday, giving her a chance to make some calls. She sent the invitation out by E-mail at noon, and though she'd requested R.S.V.P.s by the same means, some of their friends, knowing they had separate lines, started calling her with acceptances just as he returned from campus. She had to keep her voice down and keep the conversation general while he puttered in the next room.

She was pleasantly surprised when Toby Clench called, having doubted he would come. One of Kyle's students at N.Y.U. a few years ago, he'd gone on to publish a wildly successful novel, and since then his teacher's feelings had oscillated between pride and jealousy. Kyle's own novel, published six years before, had been a critical success, but it hadn't been featured on the cover of the *New York Times Book Review*, as Toby's had, nor had it been optioned by Brad Pitt's production company. But Toby's meteoric debut had certainly raised Kyle's profile, because he routinely cited his mentor in interviews.

"I'll be coming in from London that afternoon," Toby told her, "but for sure I wouldn't miss it."

"Kyle will be so pleased," Sabrina said. "I'll put you by someone sexy and smart."

"I hope that means I'll be sitting next to you," he said.

She heard Kyle's footsteps approaching the bedroom door. "We'll just have to see," she said, lowering her voice.

Kyle appeared in the doorway as she put down the receiver. "S'up?"

"Nothing." Her voice sounded high and false—the squawk of a seabird.

He smiled. "Need anything? I'm going out for a pack of smokes."

"I'm fine." How could he not notice her discomposure?

"See you in a few."

She was relieved that he hadn't noticed anything, but after the elevator door closed behind him, she wondered if he'd always been so unobservant. In class she'd often heard him invoke Henry James's prescription for writers: "Try to be someone on whom nothing is lost." He also had it on a typed index card tacked on the bulletin board over his desk.

She was pleased, though, to nab Toby for the party. That was a coup. She'd definitely seat him next to her; after all, he'd asked. And as the hostess, she figured she was entitled to sit beside the smartest and most entertaining guy at the party. She'd loved his book. Sure, it had become fashionable to say Toby's novel was overrated—she'd heard Kyle say it—but in her opinion that was just jealousy talking.

The answering machine was a problem. She kept meaning to get the service from Verizon, but for now she turned down the volume whenever she left the bedroom, worried that Kyle might overhear something about his birthday. She kept the R.S.V.P. list in the bottom drawer of her desk. Suddenly she wondered if he ever looked through her things, or, for that matter, wondered about her life beyond the sphere of this loft. She considered the few stories he'd written since they'd been living together: The women in the stories weren't terribly complex, really. There was a recurring neurotic, mendacious, narcissist type that represented his old girlfriend. And then there was the nice girl, presumably her, who the angst-ridden protagonist struggles to be worthy of. Nice, but hardly subtle or interesting. Which said more about his lack of curiosity than it did about her. She couldn't remember the last time he'd asked her about her desires and dreams and fears. She hadn't said anything at the time, reading the last couple of stories, but he actually wasn't very good with female characters.

While Kyle was out getting cigarettes, George Brasso called to accept. "But I'd rather be having an intimate dinner with you," he said.

"I'm not sure Kyle would like that."

"Does that mean you told him about us?"

"To tell you the truth, I forgot about us until just this minute," she said. They'd been classmates at Yale and they'd had a fling their first year in the city.

"You've never told him?"

"A girl needs a few secrets," she said.

"I couldn't agree more."

She heard the elevator. "I've gotta go. Kyle's back."

"Call me."

Sabrina went out to make a cup of tea, and Kyle was in the kitchen, flipping through the mail. While she stood at the counter, waiting for the water to boil, he came up behind her and wrapped one arm around her waist, groping her breast with his free hand.

"What say we take a little break?" he said.

"From what?" For some reason, she wasn't really in the mood. But as he stroked her breast, she relented. "Okay," she said, turning off the kettle and walking back to the bedroom.

"Wow," he said when they'd finished. She was almost surprised to hear his voice, so absorbed had she been in her own orgasm. She felt a little guilty, realizing she'd been thinking about George. They'd never really had any resolution to an affair that had lasted only a few months before George went off to Paris for *Newsweek*. Was she keeping her options open? George had, upon his return to New York, become a mutual friend, but somehow she'd neglected to tell Kyle about their history. Then again, she wondered why he'd never asked. She'd always been afraid the sexual tension between her and George was conspicuous, but Kyle had never once commented on it, which suddenly seemed incredibly weird. Was he that unperceptive, or did he just not care?

Two hours later she found herself increasingly irritable as she waited for him to leave for his weekly department meeting. She had a lot of party-related calls to make. With each passing minute she became more agitated. Finally she went out to see what he was doing. As nonchalantly as she could, she asked about the meeting.

"Postponed," he said cheerfully. "Haddon and Maselli are sick."

The next day, Sabrina had to fly to D.C. She worried about the phone, then decided it was better to say something than to have Kyle pick up her line or turn up the volume on the answering machine.

"Listen," she said, "I've ordered this birthday present and somebody might be calling about it. That's why I turned down the volume on the machine."

"You don't have to get me anything," he said.

Which struck her as a silly thing to say.

"Of course I do. And you sure as hell better get me something for mine. Now promise me you'll stay away from the phone."

"Cross my heart and hope to die."

The next evening, the night before the party, they stayed home and watched *Le Mépris*, Godard's adaptation of the Moravia novel. Kyle was in a Moravia phase.

"Do you ever get jealous?" she asked, lying on the couch with her legs in his lap.

He shrugged. "Not really. I trust you."

"I trust you, too," she said, "but I wouldn't want you sharing a villa in Capri with Brigitte Bardot."

"Don't worry," he said. "She must be in her seventies by now."

"Wouldn't you be worried if I were on an island with some hunky guy?"

"Probably," he said.

In the end, Kyle was surprised. He was expecting dinner à deux, tickled that the restaurant was named after a Henry James novel. When everyone jumped up from behind the banquettes, he was flabbergasted.

"You really didn't have any idea, did you?" she said.

"Not a clue," he said before happily throwing himself into the scrum of his friends, many of whom had originally been her friends.

Brom, the owner, materialized at her side with a drink. "Ketel One and soda," he said.

"You remembered."

"It's part of the job."

"So I'm just another Ketel and soda to you."

"I wouldn't say that."

This wasn't like her, this silly flirtatious banter. But he *was* cute. When they were finally seated, he leaned over and whispered in her ear that he'd be upstairs in the office if she needed anything. She nodded, then leaned toward Toby. "Do you think that a great writer, by definition, is someone who can't be surprised? Who notices everything?"

"Someone on whom nothing is lost."

"Exactly."

"Are you trying to decide whether Kyle's a great writer?"

"Maybe."

"I think you know the answer to that question."

"I do?" But he was right, of course.

As the dessert plates were being cleared, she thought it was only proper to go up and thank Brom for everything. He rose from behind his desk when she appeared in the doorway. It would seem quite wonderful later, when she recalled the moment, that he hadn't even hesitated. He'd just walked right over and taken her by the shoulders and kissed her so violently that her lips felt bruised the next day. Standing in front of the mirror that morning, she studied her swollen lips and wondered if Kyle would even notice.

As it turned out, he did eventually ask about the hickey on her collarbone, but by then it was too late.

Invisible Fences

So I come in the front door about one in the morning, after stopping to get some beer and cigarettes, and I hear these sounds from the living room. Two kinds, a low guttural growl that doesn't even sound human and a high-pitched chirping that some kind of distressed tropical bird might make but which I recognize as the love song of my wife, Susan.

"Honey?" I call.

I walk into the living room and this is what I see: Susan naked on the floor, entwined with an equally naked stranger.

"Jesus, Susan."

The man lifts his head from between her legs and regards me with mild alarm.

"You could've waited till I got back," I say.

"I'm sorry," she says breathlessly. "I guess I got carried away."

Meanwhile, the man—I think he said his name was Marvin—puts his hand on the back of her head and directs her back to her task.

Trying to get over my pique, I kneel down on the floor beside them.

"You get those Newport Lights?" he asks, thrusting his hips into Susan's face.

Sometimes I think the difference between what we want and what we're afraid of is about the width of an eyelash.

It's amazing what human beings get accustomed to—how quickly the bizarre, the absurd and the perverse can become routine. People have become accustomed to torture, or so I've read, bonded with their tormentors, the wielders of pliers and electricity.

It happens gradually. Maybe one day you get high with another couple and there's a certain amount of joking and talk, and the next thing you know, the guy's making out with your wife and you're kind of freaked-out about it. You and his wife go at it a little, and when you look up, he's massaging your wife's breast. At that point you break it up. Enough is enough. But later you find yourself thinking about the man's hand on your wife's breast. I don't know—could you imagine something like that? I'm just throwing it out as a hypothetical. A possible scenario.

The thing is, I consider myself a pretty normal guy. I manage the bookstore in the Sunset Mall. My parents are still married. My wife, Susan, is a lawyer who works for the city. We have two kids, Cara and Bucky, both of them baptized at the First Episcopal, and while I can't say we go to church every Sunday, we're there for the big holy days. We live in a place where people ask on first meeting what church you go to, a city that has far more churches than saloons. Most of the Bibles in the country are published here, and so are most of the country songs. We also have more strip clubs and massage parlors and adult bookstores than you'd think possible, all tucked away downtown, just off the cloverleaf where the interstate hits the bypass. Locals will tell you it's all out-of-towners at those places, but I'm not convinced. You might even make a case for some kind of correlation between all the pay sex and all these churches, though I wouldn't make it in public, since there's also a hell of a lot of guns around here. I myself have a '38 revolver between the mattress and the box spring and a twelve-gauge Remington pump in the gun cabinet, which would be considered about average. So far I haven't used the '38 for anything, but it makes me feel safer knowing it's there, even though the statistics tell me otherwise. I use the twelve-gauge for ducks; every winter I go with some college buddies down to Reelfoot Lake. We spend four days drinking and shooting, bitching about our wives and our jobs, talking about fish we've caught, and others we should've caught, and occasionally about the girls we've nailed, but more often about the ones who got away.

Sometimes, deep into the sour mash after a morning of freezing in the duck blind, things can get pretty confessional. But in my experience, men are more circumspect when it comes to their sex lives than women are. Susan once let me hide in the closet while she threw a baby shower for her friend Genevra, and all I can say is, it scared me, the shit they were saying. Length and width and how many times. Not that it didn't turn me on, especially when Susan started bragging on me. I'm sitting there next to the dusty-smelling vacuum cleaner with a hard-on. But these women were just, I don't know, clinical, whereas men speak in generalities and hypotheticals. Like, *Hey, tell you what. I'd love to do that waitress down at the Trace.* Or, *What about that Penélope Cruz, whooee! I could wear her out.* As for me, I've never been so shitfaced as to share any intimate love details with the boys. Not that I haven't fantasized and even talked with Susan about sharing more than the details with my buddies. Susan gets it—she thinks it's sexy. But there's fantasy and there's reality. Even when you're pushing the frontier between them— especially when you're pushing it—it's important to know where the one leaves off and the other begins. I may be a pervert, but I'm not an idiot. I can't help wondering, though, what happens late at night on their living room floors.

So anyway, on Friday nights Susan's mom takes the kids and we head out on the town. We go different places, often hitting three or four spots in a night. Susan dresses up, puts on makeup and her finest lingerie. Usually I buy the lingerie, or we pick it together out of the Victoria's Secret catalog. "Do you like the pink, or the black and white," she'll ask, standing in front of the mirror. She has a superb little body. Petite but voluptuous—and I don't mean fat. I mean five four, with curves like Daytona. I still can't look at her breasts without my breath catching in my throat. Sometimes I get faint seeing them suddenly. I mean, really. A few of the girls at work have asked her if she has implants, not that they're so big—she sort of fluctuates between B and C—but because they just seem a little too good to be true. Sometimes I can't believe they're mine, so to speak. It must be kind of like marrying money. You think, Whoa, what did I do to deserve these? When I saw guys looking at them, it made me proud. Maybe that was the beginning of something. Sometimes the guys look in a lecherous way, but more often they're secretive and pained, like dogs trying to sneak up on a garbage can. It's like, God, what I wouldn't give to get a good look at those, to stroke them, to put my mouth on those nipples. I admit it: I encourage her to wear tops that show her off, buy her tight little low-cut things.

So, on Friday nights I get home as quick as I can. I'm usually at the house by six, but on this particular night I'm a few minutes late. Darlene, the baby-sitter, is hovering by the front door with her jacket on, all antsy to smoke a cigarette and drive over to her boyfriend's house. My friend Hal always talks about how hot she is and how he'd be happy to drive her home sometime, but I don't know, it's not my thing. She has unnaturally yellow hair and a deep cavernous navel that she displays at all times, winter and summer, beneath short little T-shirts and halters. Sometimes I can't believe I entrust my kids to this little tramp, but so far they haven't broken any bones, collected any tattoos or ingested anything too terribly toxic on her watch. On the other hand, why is Cara lying on the floor, sobbing?

"Bongo saw another dog and he chased it," Darlene says. "I tried to catch him, but he got away."

Appearing in the doorway, trailing her blanket, Cara confirms this. "Bongo run away."

"He'll come back," I say.

Every once in a while he gets so worked up by some dog in the street that he forgets about the Invisible Fence that encircles the property. Getting zapped as he crosses the line makes him even crazier. Fucking Bongo.

"Darlene says he'll get smooshed by a car."

"Where's your brother?"

"Darlene says dogs can't go to heaven."

"Honey, Darlene's no expert on heaven," I say.

Susan's still at work, so I fire up a box of Kraft mac and cheese for the kids, the leftovers of which I eat myself, then pack them up for their big night at grandma's, Bucky with his Game Boy, his Pokémon cards and figures, his Spongebob pajamas, two pairs of jeans, two T-shirts and two sweatshirts, one that says Vanderbilt and the other UT, equal time for Susan's alma-mater and mine. Cara packs her own Hello Kitty backpack: Barbie night-gown, Barbie and Chrissie dolls, the usual stuff.

"Come on, come on," I say.

"I don't want to go to Grammy's," Bucky says.

"Sure you do," I say. "You always have fun at Grammy's."

"Her house smells funny."

"What about Bongo?" Cara whines.

I've forgotten about that. "Okay, let's go find Bongo."

We walk out front and look up and down the street, though I don't really expect to see the crazy mutt—the last time he ran off, we got a call two days later from the next town over. Bongo's a wanderer. He's also a biter, which is why we always make sure he's out in the backyard before we bring anybody over on Friday nights.

"I'm sure Bongo will come home soon," I say, but Cara's still weepy when I drive them over to Susan's mother's house.

"What have you kids got planned for tonight?" Susan's mother asks me after we have planted the kids in front of the TV.

"Just going to have a bite and hit the town."

"I think it's great the way you two have your together time. It's important to keep the romance alive. Some couples, the kids come along, they just let the spark go out." I'm afraid she's going to start talking about her ex, Susan's dad, an epic horndog who has achieved sainthood since he succumbed to lung cancer a few years back.

"We're trying to keep it fresh," I say.

"It takes work," she says. "You can't just take it for granted. Buck and I, we had our problems, Lord knows. But every Saturday night he'd take me to dinner at the club."

If I were her, I wouldn't bring up the club; there's a famous story about my father-in-law and one of the waitresses. "He was a hell of a guy, old Buck."

"I'm not saying he was perfect."

She's getting misty-eyed now, and it's absolutely imperative to change the subject before I get the full-blown eulogy. "He was smart enough to marry you at least."

"I have my faults, too. Believe me, I know."

"Not in my book." I give her a big hug, being careful not to crush her prominent calcium-deficient bones. "You've been great to us."

"I'm only glad I can be here to help."

"You know how grateful we are," I say. "And the kids love it, too."

As if to disprove this assertion, Bucky intercepts me on the front step and attaches himself to my leg, and it takes a good ten minutes to get him settled down again.

Back at the house, Susan is tweaking herself in front of her vanity.

"Turn around."

She puts her arms down and stares at herself in the mirror.

"Susan? Let me see."

She's wearing a low-cut white cotton halter with low-rider Diesel jeans. Sexy without being threatrical. Her makeup seems subdued. I feel like she could go heavier on the eyeliner. Finally, she stands up and walks to the closet.

"What's the matter?"

She stands at the closet door. "Nothing," she says. "Long day. I'm a little tired."

"We can take care of that," I say, showing her the gram vial I copped at lunchtime.

"Maybe later," she says. She's still standing there, looking into the closet as if at some profound vista.

I walk over behind her, put my hands on her shoulders and rub her neck and her delts. There's nothing to see in the closet except two rows of hanging clothes, hers and mine. "Sure you don't want a little pick-me-up?"

"What the hell," she says, turning around and flashing a wan smile. I tap some onto the fleshy part between her thumb and forefinger. She huffs it up and holds out the other hand. "Have you seen Bongo?" she asks.

"He broke out," I say, generously anointing her other hand. "Remind me to turn off the fence so he can get back in."

By the time we get to the Corral, a sprawling C and W dance hall about ten miles west on the interstate, Susan seems to have shaken her funk. We order a couple of platinum margaritas and survey the crowd. We haven't been here in four or five months. Last time, Susan picked up a guy who was a lineman for the phone company, but he was shifaced by the time she got him out of there and ended up puking in the parking lot, which is where we left him, sprawled over the hood of his truck, drooling on his snakeskin Justins. Earlier, he'd been telling Susan all about the boots, which he'd just bought that afternoon at the outlet in Gallatin.

"Lone Ranger at four o'clock," I shout over Tim McGraw's "Cowboy in Me," indicating a guy down the bar in a shiny orange leather jacket who's been checking her out.

"Let's dance," she says.

"Okay." I finish my drink and lead her out to the floor. We shimmy to Carrie Underwood's "Before He Cheats," or rather, she shimmies and I sway. I look around to see if Susan's got an audience, and sure enough, Mr. Leather Jacket is standing at the edge of the dance floor, watching. At the end of the song, I lean over and whisper in her ear. "Keep dancing," I say. I turn and walk away, heading to the men's room, even though I don't really have to go. Linger there and fix my hair in the mirror, then go back to the bar and order another margarita, forcing myself not to look over to the dance floor until I've paid for my drink and taken a long swallow. Sure enough, now he's dancing with Susan, grinding up against her while Alison Krauss sings "Simple Love." I feel a tingling buzz that's like the first wave of a coke rush.

What can I say? It turns me on watching Susan turn other men on. Is that so hard to understand?

I settle in at a table where I can occasionally glimpse them through the crowd. Susan eventually spots me and maneuvers her partner closer so I have a better view, then starts making out with him. I mean really sucking face. This guy can't believe his luck. Which is, strangely enough, just how I feel.

But then, just to torture me, she drifts back into the sea of bodies until I can't see either one of them anymore. It's making me crazy. I wait a few minutes, then circle the place, but I can't see them anywhere. What the hell? I look everywhere. Did she take him out to the parking lot? On a sudden inspiration I bolt for the men's room. Sometimes she trash-talks about doing some guy in the men's room because she know it's a turn-on in theory, but in real life that's a taboo, one of the boundaries we've established. When you're playing outside the regular borders, it's important to have rules and boundaries. We've learned that the hard way.

I stop at the men's room door and take a deep breath, trying to compose myself, to think what I'll do if I find them in there. I push the door open. A couple of good old boys in Stetsons, propping themselves up against the urinals. No one in the stalls, which is a relief, I think.

I finally find her at the bar, alone, sucking down a margarita.

"So?"

She shakes her head. "Let's get out of here."

In the car, she says, "He told me he wanted me to meet his mother."

"He must get a lot of pussy with that line."

"Actually, I think he was serious."

"So where to?"

"Let's go to Tini's," she says.

"You sure?" I'm still sober enough to feel some trepidation about Tini's. The last time we were there, somebody got stabbed, although we didn't actually see the fight.

"If we're going to go for it, let's just go for it." Her earlier diffidence seems to have evaporated. "Turn it up," she says, when "Mr. Bright Eyes" comes on Lightning 100.

It's early for Tini's, but the Friday-night house band's already playing. We settle in at a table and order drinks. Mostly old drunks and a few friends of the band so far. A fat mama in a gold bustier calls out, "Tell it!" and "Play it!" in between choruses. It would be easy to imagine these losers are playing the same song over and over, the same twelve bars on an interminable loop, but every once in a while a lyric emerges or the guitarist cuts loose and at some point I make out Sonny Boy Williamson's "Fattening Frogs for Snakes."

Then I see him approaching, rolling like an aspiring pimp, gold chains bouncing on a voluminous white T-shirt. He grabs the empty chair at our table and flips it around, then straddles the back of it. He's not much more than twenty, if that, very dark-skinned.

"I seen you here before," he says.

"That's possible," I say.

"Yeah, I seen you all right."

"I'm Susan, and this is Dean."

It's true: I remember him. We partied with one of his friends.

"I'm dry," he says.

"What are you drinking," I ask.

"Yak and Coke."

"I'll get you one."

"Hennessy," he says, getting cocky.

I look over at Susan to see if it's okay. You need to have signals; you've got to be able to communicate. But she seems fine. In fact, she seems more than fine, with that blurry, lascivious look on her face. How the hell much did she drink at the Corral anyway?

I'm waiting at the bar, listening to "Little Red Rooster," when I hear three little pops. It's like the witnesses always say when you see them on the eleven o'clock news; it's like firecrackers, or maybe somebody snapping a whip outside the door, so I don't even think about it until a young guy with a reddish Afro in a puffy black parka comes running in the bar, shouting, and even though I can't make out a word of what he's saying, the place starts clearing out. Suddenly, Susan and the kid are beside me.

"There's been a shooting in the parking lot," she says. "Derek needs a ride." She doesn't quite wink at me, but she's got that little smirk on her face.

Outside, I catch a glimpse of legs on the ground between the legs of the onlookers, bright white Nikes splayed on the pavement.

"I don't need that shit," the kid says as we're driving away. "You know what I'm sayin'?"

"I hear you."

"You can drop me on Broadway."

"Whatever," I say.

"Or you could come to our place," Susan says. "We could party."

"I got a bottle of Courvoisier," I say.

"XO?"

"I think. It might be VSOP."

"Y'all got any reefer?"

"We've got some fine bud, plus some killer blow."

He seems to be considering the offer, weighing the pros and cons. I try to find him in the rearview, but it's too dark.

"Where y'all's crib?"

"We're over in Green Hills."

He snorts. "More like the white hills."

"Len Simmons lives down the street," Susan says. I turn toward her and roll my eyes, but she's not looking at me. Jesus Christ, I think. But the kid seems impressed that we have a Heisman winner in the nabe.

"Not bad," he says, surveying the house from the vantage of the entry hall.

"Yak and Coke?"

"To start with."

"Susan will show you around," I say, handing him a Baggie with buds and papers.

When I return with the drinks, they're sitting beside each other on the living room couch. Derek is sealing the joint with his tongue.

"What's a crib like this set you back?"

"We bought in '01, back before the big run-up."

He lights up the joint, inhales and hands it to Susan. "I'm gonna get me a house like this."

"It's a great investment."

Susan inhales deeply on the joint while I chop the coke on the coffee table.

Derek nods at me. "We oughta call Len Simmons."

"His daughter goes to school with our little boy."

"That wife of his, she look like she know how to get down."

"She's hot," I say, handing him a length of straw.

"White folks is all about the powder," he says. "Where I comes from, s'all about the rock. You ever smoke that rock?" He leans over and snorts a couple of lines, then hands the straw to Susan.

She gathers her hair behind her head and starts to lean forward. "Would you hold my hair?" she asks.

"No problem." He holds her hair as she crouches down over the coffee table. I've always found this incredibly sexy. When she comes back up, she strokes his arm and kisses him on the cheek. I get the feeling he's just beginning to get a sense of the possibilities.

"What kind of party y'all got in mind here?"

"Just hanging out, getting down," I say.

"'Cause I ain't into no dudes."

"You're a ladies' man," Susan says.

I shake my head. "Me, neither," I say.

"I ain't ridin' no trike."

"I hear you."

Derek scratches his chin contemplatively. "We need some tunes."

"Coming right up."

I figure *The Black Album* is a pretty safe choice. Marvin Gaye or Al Green might just be pushing it, at least to start. Susan's bending down over the coffee table. Derek takes her hair in one hand and puts the other beneath her breast. This time when she comes up, she starts to kiss him. I hold my breath, standing beside the sound system. This is no time to call attention to my presence. I wish I could say why this thrills me, why I love seeing my wife sticking her tongue in this stranger's mouth, especially when he has skin the color of French-roast coffee. They make out for three or four minutes while I stand there. Then I see Susan going for his belt. By now I have inched a few feet closer, but she has her back to me, blocking most of my view, as she slides his pants down below his knees. At this point I have to remember to keep breathing. Still in stealth mode, I move around the coffee table to improve my angle.

I hear Bongo just moments before I see him; he's barking frantically even before he launches himself at this man who is wrestling with Susan on the couch. The ensuing racket is terrifying, Susan screaming, Derek cursing, Bongo snarling and barking, until he comes flying in my direction, yelping as he lands at my feet. I grab hold of him as he tries to make another run at Derek.

"Motherfucker bit me. Jesus Christ. I'm bleeding. That fuckin' dog bit my ass."

Susan is examining his thigh, which seems to have been the part of his body that actually sustained the wound.

"Fuckin' crazy," he says. "Where'd that racist motherfucker come from?"

"I think we need to get him to the emergency room," Susan says to me. Bongo's still barking and lunging as I clutch his collar.

"You people are way fucked-up," Derek says as we lay rubber out of the cul-de-sac. "What the fuck's wrong with y'all?"

There's not much to say to this, so far as I can see. I hear a sniffling sound from Susan's side of the car and I see that she's crying.

"Fuckin' crazy white folks."

"It's true," she says.

I feel like pointing out that he was down with the program until Bongo bit his ass, but I decide to keep my counsel. I mean, nobody was holding a gun to his head, were they?

Derek can't contain his indignation. "Whassup with you people? You pick up strange white dudes, too, or is this some Mandingo thing?"

"No, it's not." Susan wipes her nose and sniffles. "It's not just— It's both."

She looks over at me, as if trying to read something in my face.

"I think maybe, I don't know, Dean likes it better when it's, you know, a black guy."

"Me? What are you talking about? Don't put that on me. You started that."

"If I did, it was only because I felt like you wanted me to."

"I never said that."

"You never complained, either."

"And that gave you license to go for it," I say. "Which is obviously what you wanted."

"Deeply fucked-up, man."

"Hey," I say, "we never forced anybody."

He leans forward in the backseat and slaps me on the head. "Shut the fuck up," he says. "I want to hear what she say." To Susan, he says, "You into this shit?"

She looks over at me, and I don't like what I'm seeing.

"I don't know. I guess I've gotten used to it."

"Gotten *used* to it?" I can't believe this. She's completely rewriting history.

"You know, after a while it was just . . . something we did."

"Give me a fucking break," I say. "You love getting fucked by strange men. And you really love getting fucked by strange black men."

Derek smacks me again, harder this time. "Shut up and keep your eyes on the fuckin' road. And show the lady some goddamn respect."

We're coming up on the hospital.

"How long's this shit been goin' on?"

Susan is slumped over in the front seat, as if she's suddenly gone boneless. I notice the little blond Kelly doll sprawled, arms and legs akimbo, at her feet. I'm getting fed up with this inquisition. I mean, what the hell difference does it make how long it's been going on, and what does he care?

"I can tell you exactly," Susan says. "It was after Dean . . ." Her voice catches and a sob escapes her pursed lips. "It was after he found out about something I'd done."

"Somethin' you done? Or someone you done?"

"Well, yeah, someone I'd slept with."

"What are you talking about?" I say. "What does that have to do with anything?"

"Oh come on. As if you don't remember."

"I don't know what the hell you're talking about."

"I'm *talking* about you finding out about me and Cleve Thompson."

"What the fuck does that have to do with anything? And why are we talking about this now?"

"Come on, Dean. That's what really started this. How long was it between you finding out about Cleve and you telling me to pick up that man at the Last Exit."

"That was like— That was way later. And you're the one who brought up the idea of coming on to that guy."

"Oh please."

"Even if it was my idea, which it wasn't, I didn't hear you protesting real loud."

She turns and gives me a look, which is worse than anything that's led up to it. "No, you didn't," she says. "But let's at least all be honest about our motivations here, for a change."

None of us says much of anything as we wait in the ER. I give them my credit card because Derek doesn't have any insurance and it seems we're pretty much responsible for his being here. I'm wondering if the guy who got shot at Tini's came through here. Across from us is a rail-thin country boy in a bloody NASCAR T-shirt, clutching a bloody towel to his neck, sitting beside his fat mother, who's wearing a voluminous pastel sweatsuit. "I done told you," she says several times over the next ten minutes.

Finally, after they take Derek in to be stitched up, I turn to Susan. "You don't really believe what you said back there," I say. "That our . . . little adventures . . . that I'm, what? Punishing you?"

"For Christ's sake, Dean. Wake up."

Forty minutes later, I'm dropping Derek off at a bar on Sixth Street.

"Why'n cha come on with me," he says to Susan.

To my amazement, she seems to be considering the offer. "I should."

"Give old numbnuts here somethin' to think about."

"I appreciate the offer."

"You know where to find me," he says, climbing out of the back and slamming the door.

I can't imagine what to say now. Neither, apparently, can Susan. We drive past the bright neon signs of one franchise after another in silence. It's a little past one. A gibbous harvest moon hangs over the interstate, leaking an orange glow into the surrounding sky. It's a beautiful sight, even now.

I look across at Susan. A shiny tear moves down her cheek. "What?" I say.

"I was just thinking of the first time."

I almost ask the first time for what, but I don't. That would be hostile. Instead, I pull over in front of the Outback Steakhouse.

"You remember?"

"Of course I do."

"We drove up to your uncle's place on the lake. In that terrible car of yours."

I remember all right. It was a Friday night, the week before graduation. We drove up to Center Lake in my old Subaru, which had a hole in the muffler and smelled inside of gas. The mattress in the bunk bed at the shack smelled like mildew, but my new sleeping bag had a fresh, synthetic smell that was eventually canceled out by the heady, deeply organic funk of our mingled secretions—the first time I'd encountered the smell of sex. I remember the furious creaking of the rusty old bed and the lapping of waves on the shore outside and, eventually, afterward, Susan's muffled sniffles. I didn't know what to think except that somehow I'd failed. "What's the matter?" I'd finally asked. "I'm fine," she'd said, wrapping herself around me in the sleeping bag, her cheek wet against my shoulder.

"You thought I was unhappy," she says now, as if she's reading my mind.

"What was I supposed to think?"

"I was crying because it was perfect, and because it would never be the first time again."

I shake my head and shrug.

"I was crying because I didn't want to ever lose you, but I knew that if we stayed together, sooner or later we would hurt each other."

"You didn't lose me," I say hopefully, reaching over and taking her hand.

"Yeah," she says, wiping the tear from her face. "Actually, I think I did."

"We can go back."

Susan shakes her head and stares straight ahead out the windshield.

I look out, too, trying to remember what made it a harvest moon, and wondering if it was waxing or waning. Of course I remember when I found out about Cleve Thompson. I thought I'd lose my mind. I thought my heart would burst with rage and grief. I couldn't sleep for days. I imagined the two of them in every possible position, in every nuance of lust and carnality. I raged, wept, broke her entire collection of Staffordshire figurines, demanded an explanation. She sent the children to her mother's and I took three days off work. I couldn't eat, and when I did, I vomited. I asked if she still loved me and didn't believe her when she said she did. How could she fuck him if she loved me? I couldn't reconcile the two facts. I thought I would die of heartbreak. I'd always believed I would be her only.

So I made her tell me everything. I was tortured by visions of her treachery, by my own roiling, filthy imagination. The reality could hardly be worse, I figured. I demanded more and more details. I needed to picture her, with him, in the explicit postures of betrayal. I made her repeat and expand on the sordid details, asking questions, demanding more and more specificity, until I could see it all, or believed I could, as clearly as a porn clip, until I could almost imagine it was something I'd created for my own pleasure . . . until we both realized that the actual circumstances would never be enough to match the images in my head.

I needed more.

The March

February 15, 2003

Corrine had agreed to meet Washington and Veronica at the diner on Fifty-second Street, a place they'd come to for hamburgers on Saturday or brunch on Sunday when they were living in the neighborhood back in the eighties. It had been more than a decade since she'd set foot there, and the glazed apple pies and coconut cakes under their plastic domes seemed like museum displays from the distant era of her lost youth. But now it was jammed with cops—she hadn't seen this many uniforms since her days at the soup kitchen downtown, feeding cops and firefighters and san men and the steelworkers who had come together in the smoking ruins. She'd gotten to know several cops then, but the cohort here today seemed less benign, their faces tight, closed and bolted against fraternization. That moment of solidarity, of strangers comforting one another in the streets, of stockbrokers hugging firemen and waving to cops, had already faded into history. The citizens of the metropolis were changed, though less tangibly than they might have imagined or hoped back in the time of anthrax and missing-person posters. They had, most of them, been given a glimpse of their best selves, and told themselves they wouldn't forget, or go back to the old selfish, closed-in ways. But then they'd gone back to work and the rubble had been carted away and the stock market had recovered. You woke up one morning not thinking about that terrible day, not remembering it had happened until perhaps seeing the tattered remains of an old poster on your way to lunch. And it felt good not to think about it all the damn time.

She stepped outside to wait. Already, at ten-thirty, the street was jammed with people bundled against the cold and carrying signs. ALL WE ARE SAYING IS GIVE PEACE A CHANCE. A little kid holding one that said WAR IS TERROR and his sister in a red snowsuit with her own sign: DRAFT THE BUSH TWINS. Russell had stayed home with the kids, who were working on a play for her birthday. While he shared Corrine's feelings about the imminent war, Russell was not a joiner. "I don't march," he'd said earlier that morning, showing the same kind of contrarian pride he sometimes brought to his traditional refrain of "I don't dance."

Looking south down the sidewalk for Washington and Veronica, she felt her chest tighten as she picked out a familiar figure—the loose, loping stride beneath the camel polo coat, the flopping sandy forelock, a garment bag hanging on his shoulder like a vestigial wing. She waited, paralyzed at his approach, and watched the changes ring on his unguarded visage as he recognized her, the rapid modulation from shock to wistful chagrin that preceded his public Isn't-this-a-pleasant-surprise mien.

"I might've known you'd be here," he said as he kissed her cheek.

"Actually, I was just thinking about you," she said, a statement that to her ears sounded false in its implication of surprising coincidence; it would have been true on almost any given day, despite the fact that they hadn't seen each other in more than a year—not since that snowy night in the plaza outside the New York State Theater when they'd both been on their way to see *The Nutcracker* with their respective families. By now he had occupied more time in her thoughts than he had in the flesh. They'd exchanged E-mails and he had called from Tennessee and left a message six months ago, on September 11.

"I mean, I was thinking about those days downtown, at the soup kitchen. This whole thing . . ." She waved her arm to indicate the milling crowd with their signs. "For me, it all kind of loops back to that time. The demonstration—the war."

"Yeah, I guess so," he said. "At least that's the question, isn't it? They'd have us believe that what happened back then justifies their war." He sighed. "I didn't know this was happening, actually. The march, I mean. I was just on my way to the airport and I kind of waded into this thing. I was staying up the street at a friend's place." He pointed behind him, as if to lend credence to the claim. "We sold the apartment as part of the separation agreement."

She tried not to react to this last phrase, the confirmation that he'd parted from his wife.

"You're heading back to Tennessee?"

He nodded. "Ashley's really settled in—she's going to a girls school in Nashville and seems to love it."

"That's good."

"Your kids?"

"They're fine. They're great." It seemed important to emphasize their well-being, since the children, after all, had probably been the fatal obstacles to their romance.

"How's your mom?" It felt as if she was staging these remarks for the benefit of unseen observers, but she didn't know how to break out of the formulae of polite conversation.

"Well, that's the other thing," he said. "Not so good. She's been ill. Cancer."

"Oh my God, Luke. I'm so sorry."

"It's been rough, but the prognosis is somewhat encouraging."

"She must be glad to have you there."

He shrugged and pushed his hair off his forehead—a gesture so familiar, it made her feel faint. "Making up for lost time."

"Good for you. Are you working?" He'd been between things back when they were working downtown at the soup kitchen together, trying to decide what to do with the second half of his life.

"I'm running a little fund."

"What about the book?"

"Oh God, I'd almost forgotten about that. Maybe someday. And you? What about the screenplay?"

She told him about the actor who'd optioned it, without adding that the option had just expired the week before.

"That's great. I'll be watching for it at the Cool Springs Multiplex."

The strained formality of this exchange was exhausting her. She had been ready to change her life for him, and for the last year she'd been struggling to convince herself they'd done the right thing.

For better or worse, the arrival of Washington and Veronica rescued them from the peril of intimate revelation. Corrine made the introductions, realizing as she did so that they'd been present outside the theater the night when their affair had effectively ended. Seeing her with her husband and children had awakened his conscience, and dampened his ardor. He'd told her later that he couldn't bear to be the reason for her breaking up her family.

"Sorry we're late," Veronica said. "Traffic on the Hutch. Then we had to find parking."

"The perils of the suburban couple," Washington said, still embarrassed at being yet another commuter—that, too, a result of the attack. They'd started looking at houses in Connecticut the week after.

"You look great," Veronica said to Corrine.

"So do you."

"I'd better get on out of here and try to find a cab," Luke said.

She didn't want him to leave; as awkward as this public posturing might be, she'd hoped they might find a few more minutes to talk. Suddenly she was afraid they'd never see each other again.

They stood for a moment on the sidewalk, the bitter cold infiltrating the soles of her shoes, uncertain of the form their parting should take.

He leaned over and kissed her cheek, the brush of his unruly forelock across her face excruciatingly familiar. If she'd had any doubt about his state of mind these last few minutes, she saw now that he was as miserable as she was. He managed a rueful smile before turning away and walking east. She watched as he slowly disappeared into the flow of the converging marchers.

"What's with all the fucking heat?" Washington said, nodding as four cops exited the coffee shop. Sullen, wide-bodied white guys girdled with hardware, pulling up their pants and avoiding eye contact with the civilians, they exuded the grim camaraderie of an army in enemy territory.

Corrine shook her head. Nothing seemed real to her right now, her resolve evaporating along with an animating sense of indignation about the war soon to take place six thousand miles away.

"I don't like the look of this shit," he said. "Maybe you should make your own damn sign: MY SISTER MARRIED A COP."

For a moment she didn't know what he was talking about, then she realized it was true. Her sister *had* married a cop, another improbable result of that improbable time.

It was reassuring being a part of a crowd, surrendering to its volition. They merged with the throng flowing east toward Second, marching beside a sign that said FREEZING MY ASS OFF FOR PEACE. The air was cold enough to show their breath as they pressed forward, trying to see up ahead. The Roosevelt Island tramway rose up in the distance. Corrine got clunked by a CHILDREN AGAINST WAR sign being carried by a little girl right behind her. Maybe it would have been good, she thought, for the kids to see this.

Luke had been stricken at the sight of her twins outside the theater that night. She'd seen it in his eyes. At that moment she'd known this chance encounter had doomed them, though they'd struggled to recover from it for several days of agonized discussions. It wasn't rational really, since he'd known from the beginning about her family. In fact, the plan had been to tell their spouses after Christmas.

When they finally reached Second Avenue, the march turned north, although their destination, the U.N., was some ten blocks south and east.

Washington was jumping in the air, trying to get a look ahead. "Why the fuck are we going uptown?" he said.

"They've blocked Second," a kid in a tasseled ski hat explained. "We have to go north and circle back down."

"That doesn't make sense," Corrine said.

"It makes lots of sense," Washington said, "if they're trying to keep us away from the U.N."

At times the sound of car horns was deafening. The marchers overflowed the sidewalks, filling in the gaps between vehicles like mortar, blocking the traffic aimed in the opposite direction. This was now completely unreal.

A voice from a megaphone was directing them to proceed north.

"They're trying to scatter us," said the man beside her, whose EMPTY WARHEADS sign featured caricature heads of Bush, Cheney and Rumsfeld, each one of them open, the crowns of the skulls rising on hinges.

"I like your sign," she said.

"They're trying to keep us from getting there, the bastards."

"Is this fucked-up or what?" Washington said.

Veronica said, "I'm glad we didn't bring the kids."

"Hey, it would've been educational," Washington said. "A lesson in the trampling of our motherfucking constitutional right of assembly."

"Why are they doing this?"

"A Republican governor and mayor sucking up to our president is what's going on," Washington said.

Corrine and Veronica fell into step behind him, having barely spoken in two or three months.

Veronica squeezed her glove. "How are you?"

"Fine. The kids are great."

"And you two?"

"Well, Russell took me to Bouley last night for Valentine's." She wondered where, and with whom, Luke had been last night—if there was someone in his life now, a question she'd been afraid to ask: a childhood sweetheart, some southern girl with pouffed-up hair and a syrupy accent.

"Washington cooked his famous Szechuan chicken and we opened a bottle of sparkling cider."

"That sounds nice."

"It sounds boring. But boring is better than all-nighters and strange parties, I guess. I don't know, I hate the commute and I miss the city, and those stay-at-home moms are just clones. I can't make up my mind which scares me more—the possibility that my kids won't be accepted by their peers or the possibility that they'll grow up just like them."

Corrine, meanwhile, was wondering if Luke was happy, and if she wanted him to be. Yes, of course she did. Only, she wanted him to think of her and to wonder sometimes, as she did, whether they had really done the right thing after all.

At Sixty-third Street they were greeted by a phalanx of cops, a line of barricades blocking the street. A red-faced policeman with a crescent scar on his cheek pointed his billy club north.

"What's the point of pushing us uptown?" Corrine asked him.

"Just keep moving," he said.

The next street, when they reached it, was also blocked off.

"Hey, man," Washington said, "we live on this block."

"We need ID," the cop said.

"Officer, I don't understand," Corrine said. "We're not trying to cause any trouble. We're just exercising our constitutional right of assembly and free speech."

"Just keep moving."

Washington took her arm and eased her away from the barricade.

"Why are they doing this?" she demanded. "Why are they *being* like this? They don't act this way at the Saint Patrick's Day parade."

"Exactly," Washington said, his hand still on her arm.

"Even if they're enforcing some ridiculous order," Veronica said, "they could at least be civil."

The faces of these cops reminded Corrine of the old pictures of Selma and Birmingham.

"It's an outrage, that's what it is." The speaker was a Waspy middle-aged blonde with a black velvet hair band

and a three-quarter-length mink. A bit of an anomaly in this crowd, she put Corrine in mind of an older version of Luke's ex, Sasha, whose picture she occasionally saw in the party pages of magazines.

Up ahead, the crowd was chanting raggedly, the chorus moving fitfully down the column, picked up by the marchers and passed along before it spluttered and died as they reached Sixty-fifth Street, which was also blocked off.

"This is ridiculous," Corrine said.

"It's all part of the plan," Washington replied.

"What plan?"

An old guy who was wearing a camo jacket and had long gray hair and a beard was shouting to her over the din. "They don't want us anywhere near the U.N., or the cameras."

"Who doesn't? This is America. This is New York, for God's sake. Who ordered this? The police commissioner? Our squeaky mayor? That asshole in the White House?" The injustice of it infuriated her. The idea that the attack on the city was being used to justify this dubious war was outrage enough.

Glancing up ahead, she could see a huge globe borne aloft by the crowd. About ten feet in diameter, it appeared to be made out of soft fabric.

"*Whose streets? Our streets!*"

Corrine took up the chant. Her anger was righteous and liberating. She was cold, her ears and toes prickly with numbness. If the cops were trying to incite the crowd to violence, they were doing a good job of it.

"*Whose streets? Our streets!*"

She was a peaceful person, the mother of two, but she felt like throwing something, breaking something, running amok.

"*Whose streets? Our streets!*"

Seeing all the angry faces, she had a sudden vision of chaos spreading through the city, smoke rising from the brownstones . . .

Finally at Seventy-first Street, they were herded east. As they approached First Avenue, word filtered through the crowd that it was sealed off, which made their progress seem completely futile.

Up ahead, cops on horseback towered over them. She still hoped she might find a level head, establish a dialogue, explain the purpose of their collective mission.

But she sensed anxiety rising around her, an increasing edge of anger and hysteria.

"They're making arrests!"

"Get back! They're charging!"

"You *bastards*!"

"They hit him!"

The mounted cops started moving forward as the crowd ahead of her fell back, reversing the momentum of the march, until she felt herself pushed back, up against the crowd bottled up on the sidewalk on the south side of the street. A plastic water bottle arced through the air and sailed past the head of one of the cops, shouts of distress, curses and screams rising from the intersection.

Three mounted policemen floated toward them, looming against the sky, and Corrine recognized one of them. All of a sudden the name came to her: Spinetti.

She thrust herself forward against the tide of retreat.

Sitting atop a huge chestnut mare, Spinetti held his billy club aloft, like a torch, the reins held loosely in his left hand, his eyes fixed on a point above or even beyond the crowd.

"Officer!" she shouted. "Officer Spinetti!"

The cop looked around, scanning the faces, holding his club at the ready.

A space had opened up on the street ahead of her. A boy in a puffy blue parka was lying face down on the pavement, a dark stripe glistening on his flaxen hair, which was so similar in color to her son's that despite the obvious difference in ages, she had to fight back the notion that it was her son, Jeremy, lying there, bloody, on the pavement.

She waved at Spinetti from the edge of the circle that had cleared around the boy and the horse, feeling ridiculous as soon as she did so, not sure what she intended. "It's Corrine," she said. "From the soup kitchen."

He regarded her without obvious emotion.

She didn't know what to say. She wanted to break through his blood lust and recall him to his humanity, ask him how this could happen, to remind him that when they met, their country was under attack and the citizenry looked to him and his kind to defend them. She was shivering and it felt as if her jaw were wired shut. "We fed you," she said finally. "We were proud of you."

Spinetti stared down at her implacably. Finally he lowered his club, turning his horse and moving back toward the intersection, where a dozen of his comrades were clustered.

Two women knelt down to examine the boy, who was moaning. Perhaps he had been moaning before and she hadn't noticed. Voices behind her cleared the way for a doctor coming through, and he emerged from the crowd wearing a bright orange thermal suit, silver tufts of gray hair on either side of his balding head.

Washington suddenly appeared beside her, holding her close as she shivered violently in the midday sun.

"He gave us a ride home one night," she said. "Me and Luke. He took four sugars in his coffee. I used to make him a fresh pot. I mean, what were we doing down there anyway?"

Washington was steering her west, away from the march. "Maybe so on a cold winter day you could prevent a full-scale riot from breaking out."

She was still shaking. "I want to go home," she said. "Do you think it would be okay if I just went home now?"

They offered her a ride downtown, but she didn't think she could bear even the company of friends. Finally, Washington found her a cab all the way over on Fifth. Veronica hugged her before she got in, and the cabdriver lurched manic-depressively down the avenue, braking and accelerating. She thought about the boy with the cracked head and about all the boys who would soon be bleeding and dying on the distant streets of foreign cities, and she wanted to scream at the senselessness of it all. She wanted to slap Spinetti. She wanted to draft the Bush twins. But most of all, she wanted to see Luke. She had tried to do her civic duty, but she was tired of trying to do the right thing, of always trying to be a good person and a good mother and a good wife. She wanted to live for her own desires and forget, if only for a little while, about the needs and wants of others. She wanted what *she* wanted. She wanted

Luke. She wanted to be fucked senseless. She'd always hated the expression, but now, suddenly, she understood it. At this moment, being fucked senseless was the only thing that seemed to make sense.

"You say West Broadway, miss?"

"West Broadway, yes. At the corner of Reade."

As they approached her building, a shaft of sunlight pierced the windshield, momentarily blinding her. For years, this part of the city had been gloomy at this time of the afternoon, entombed in shadow. This was what they called "a silver lining."

Summary Judgment

Everyone imagines it's all about blow jobs, or esoteric skills practiced in the more exclusive brothels of Europe and Asia. But other arts can be just as important to an ambitious woman who is determined to be the wife of a wealthy and powerful man. No one seems to consider how difficult it is to hold the interest of these demanding, distractable males, particularly after one has passed the first blush of youth.

Alysha de Sante was smitten with Billy Laube long before they met; she had already researched his family and his fortune in the days before Mary Trotter's dinner party, and after sitting beside him all evening she was fairly certain that she'd ignited a flame within his barrel chest. Knowing of his fondness for blood sport, she told him how much she loved shooting, and while she hated to brag, she was considered a very good shot indeed. Everyone said so. She had dropped the names of mutual acquaintances and other grandees and had also managed to convince him that it was his idea to invite her to his midtown corporate headquarters to see the art collection, which she had already researched quite thoroughly. She just adored Remington, she told him, so vigorous and masculine, naming qualities that, she hinted, she also appreciated in a tycoon. Remington was just so *American*—something that, as a European, she found terribly romantic. She had spoken knowledgeably as well about his business, while implying that she herself was burdened with the responsibility of tending to a significant family fortune.

Mary Trotter owed Alysha, who had gotten the Trotters invited to Blenheim the previous summer, and had been happy to seat her next to the recently divorced timber heir. After insisting that Mary recite the guest list, Alysha had decided against asking her to remember to use the title Contessa on her place card, after discovering that two European couples, including Lord and Lady Beecroft, had been invited. She had learned to be cautious in this regard; although she had two separate claims to the title, neither was quite beyond reproach. Alysha's mother had once been married to an Italian count and, furthermore, her second-to-last husband, Frederick de Sante, had also been a count, although, in fact, the elderly de Sante, it turned out, was still married to his second wife when Alysha called a priest to his sickbed to perform the wedding service. The prior wench had ended up with most of the count's estate, after an ugly legal battle; having lost three houses and two apartments, Alysha was damned if she'd give up the name as well. She had continued to use it during her next marriage to Sam Grossman, heir to an Atlanta-based retail empire. Sam himself had been perfectly comfortable with her decision to keep the name, even if certain third parties had chosen to be malicious.

Everyone knew her as Alysha de Sante, and it would have been confusing were she to have changed her name. The fact that Sam had been Jewish had nothing to do with it. Billy Laube, who'd recently moved east from Denver, knew none of this, and Alysha was eager to protect him from unpleasant gossip and give him an opportunity to form his own impressions.

Laube's grandfather was one of those giants who had won the West, a self-made financier with an uncanny knack for buying up vast tracts of wilderness that just happened to lie directly in the path of the advancing railroad. The Laube Corporation, of which Billy was president, was now a sprawling conglomerate with interests in timber, paper and chemicals. And unlike most of the local tycoons, he stood well over six feet, with a broad-shouldered athletic build, a thick mane of steel gray hair and—or so it seemed to Alysha—a kind of straight shooting, curmudgeonly frontier manner. His rough edges were charming—much as stubble can be attractive on the face of a younger man.

Like many rich men, he seemed to have a minor obsession with household economy. "My daughter spent four thousand dollars on a dress last month," he complained after she had asked him if he thought her own dress wasn't perhaps just a bit too low-cut. "Something she can apparently wear only once. I never in my life spent more than a thousand dollars on a suit, and I keep them for years." He held up the sleeve of his navy suit as if to demonstrate, and indeed the edge of the sleeve was frayed, the buttonholes fake. While the European men of her acquaintance tended to have their clothes custom-made, and often, she had learned to appreciate the shabby, frugal aesthetic that characterized a certain venerable subset of the American plutocracy. A mountain man by way of Deerfield and Yale, Laube had clearly taken his sartorial cues from the preppy New Englanders. It was all very charming; and later, she believed, she would have plenty of time to take him to Huntsman or Anderson-Sheppard.

"I don't believe there's any reason for young women to spend that kind of money on clothing," she told him, truly believing that the advantages of youth should be handi-capped; it wasn't fair that an unlined face and buoyant bust should be further enhanced by a couture gown.

"It's ridiculous is what it is," he said. "Not so long ago, you could get a new Buick for less than that."

"I think it's important to set limits for young people," Alysha said with feeling, indignant at the thought of this girl squandering the family fortune.

"Maybe you're right," he said. "I'll have a talk with her, goddamn it. Four thousand dollars for a piece of cloth."

"Well, I'm sure it was lovely," she said.

In response, he made a noise somewhere between a growl and a grunt, a sound she would come to know well.

When he failed to call, she wasn't discouraged. Billy Laube was one of those busy, absentminded men who often got caught up in their own affairs. Alysha felt certain that she could succeed if given a second chance. She was on the board of the ballet, and it occurred to her that Billy would be the perfect honoree for their fall gala. Although the ballet was not among the many organizations to which his company doled out donations, he had yet to be adopted by any of the other high-profile charities since arriving in New York. The other girls thought it was genius, except for Laurie Greenspan, who was new to the board.

"But what has Billy Laube ever done for the ballet?"

"The point is," Trish Baldwin told her, "what can he do for us now? As the honoree, he'll buy at least two tables for fifty each and *tout le monde* is curious to meet him."

Now she just had to convince Billy. She went through the proper channels, having the ballet secretary call the vice-president in charge of corporate giving at Laube, and eventually she followed up with Billy himself, calling from the ballet office to make it all the more official. She reminded him, briefly, of their recent encounter and then proceeded to the business at hand, her tone suggesting they were both very busy people and she wouldn't be bothering him except on a matter of great interest.

"The *ballet*?"

"Last year we honored Felix Rohatyn, and the previous year it was Bob Pittman," she explained. "It's one of the most important events on the social calendar."

"Well, I'm flattered, Miss de Sante, but I can't for the life of me understand why you would want to honor me. I'm hardly an aficionado of the ballet."

"Really? I never would've guessed. Over the years your company has been very generous to our organization."

"We have?"

"I don't suppose a man with so many corporate and charitable interests could possibly keep track of every single one of them," she said. Indeed, she was counting on that fact. "But we appreciate your support."

"There must be other fellows more—"

"I'd consider it a great personal favor if you'd consider it," she said, adopting an entirely different tone, which was meant to suggest need, vulnerability and promise. And by the time they hung up, she had his commitment.

After waiting a week, Alysha called to suggest a meeting to discuss the event. When it came time to pick the venue, he deferred to her. "Well, there's always Le Cirque," she said. When he didn't immediately make some noise of recognition, she reconsidered. Le Cirque might be a little flashy, a little Euro, a little feminine for a macho guy like himself—the realm of lunching ladies. Its masculine counterpart was '21,' the former speakeasy, exactly the kind of place where a lumber baron with a prep school tie would feel right at home.

"Let's go to '21,'" she said. "Bruce always gives me a good table."

Billy said he wasn't particular about where he sat and was delighted to let her make the reservation, which she did immediately. In fact, since the death of her last husband, she had been relegated to the middle or even the back room of '21,' but she certainly wasn't going to let that happen again. Normally, she would have her secretary make the call, but in this case she called herself and insisted on speaking directly to Bruce, the maître d'. It was all she could do to keep her voice pleasant after spending ten minutes on hold.

"Bruce, this is the Contessa de Sante. How nice to hear your voice. It seems ages since I've been in. I would like a table for two at one p.m. this coming Thursday. I will be dining with Billy Laube, who is very particular about where he sits. He would prefer one of the first banquettes, preferably the corner by the door."

"Of course we will do our very best to accommodate Mr. Laube."

At the restaurant, Alysha introduced the mogul to the maître d'. "This is my dear friend Bruce, who's one of the most important men in New York. I want you to promise me you'll take care of Billy now that he's a New Yorker."

Bruce took Billy's hand and said, "Good to see you again, Mr. Laube."

"Always a pleasure," said Billy.

After they were seated, Alysha pointed out to him that their table at the front of the room was the best in the house. She surveyed the surroundings from her privileged perch in the red leather banquette and waved to a handsome silver-haired man in a form-fitting pinstriped suit at the center table.

"That's Curt Vetters, a very good friend of mine. He used to be terribly in love with me. When I was married to my late husband, he would always tell me he wanted to run away with me. He was a very naughty man, all hands. He just bought a football team, I forget which one. I'm afraid I don't know very much about American sports."

"Well, I don't know much about ballet," Billy said, "so that makes us even. I can't quite believe I let you talk me into this thing."

"Don't worry. I will teach you everything you need to know. You must be careful, when you come to New York, not to fall in with the wrong people. It's important to have the right advice," she said, reaching over and squeezing his hand.

"I believe I'm in good shape there," he said, smiling and looking her directly in the eye before turning away to take the menu.

The following week he invited her to La Grenouille for dinner. Moments after she put the phone down, it rang again, and she picked it up, her personal assistant having disappeared for the moment.

"Alysha, I've left you half a dozen messages," her accountant said, sounding exasperated. "It's absolutely crucial that we resolve the situation with the Southampton house."

"I'm sorry, Saul, I've only just returned from Paris."

"The bank's moving to foreclose. Unless we come back to them with some kind of plan, they'll file for summary judgment next month. We're four months overdue on the mortgage payments, and now they tell me the Realtor claims you've turned down three offers in that same period."

"They weren't offers, darling; they were insults."

"Alysha, we don't have the luxury of sneering, not when you owe the bank thirty million dollars. The Realtor says the last offer was for twenty-seven, and that you refused to counter."

"The house is worth at least thirty-five and you know it. It was designed by Stanford White, for heaven's sake. You know perfectly well we paid twenty-five for it three years ago, and look at what the market's done since then."

"You overpaid, Alysha. Sam got in a pissing match with Chip Rhodes."

"How dare you speak about my husband that way?"

"I apologize, but honestly, Alysha, we're running out of options here. We've got to liquidate something. What about the art?"

It was true: She had some valuable artwork, but she continued to think of it as the cash in her sock drawer, the last line of defense between herself and destitution, and she wasn't ready to admit that things had reached that stage of crisis. The artwork had been bought at auctions in New York and in Europe, and what hadn't gone to the residences had been shipped to a warehouse in Switzerland, her hedge against the uncertainties of widowhood. Though her late husband had kept her on a rather tight leash when it came to personal expenses, he had relinquished to her the traditional female realm of household management and decor. She had formed a company, which she'd then hired to redo all of their houses. Sam had sometimes grumbled about the cost, but he'd left the details to Alysha. Some of the furniture and paintings that she and her decorators had acquired in Europe went directly into storage, a little nest egg she considered herself more than entitled to. After all, Sam's nasty children would be wildly wealthy in their own right, the income from the Grossman trust passing directly to the children upon his death. As things turned out, she only wished she'd put away more.

It had been war between Alysha and the children from the day their father proposed to her. They repeated all sorts of vile rumors and even dug up the certificate from her first marriage, to the polo player, which she hadn't told him about because it had been annulled. She only thanked God they hadn't found out about Riyadh.

Alysha wasn't one to leave an attack unanswered. She used to scrutinize their credit-card bills, which, naturally, came to her husband, and point out extravagant expenditures. Sonja was a tomboy who spent millions on horses—a mousy plain Jane, whom no one could accuse of spending too much on her wardrobe. She had a house in Millbrook, where all her horsy friends gathered on weekends. Her brother, Alex, was supposedly an art dealer, with a gallery in Chelsea underwritten by his father.

Alysha had liked to call Alex at some advanced hour, like noon, while her husband was in the room. "Oh, darling, I'm sorry, are you still sleeping? I'm so sorry I woke you. Go back to sleep." And she would hold the phone as Sam growled about the laziness of his offspring and Alex shouted, uselessly, that he'd been awake for hours.

She was still bitter about the trust agreement. She'd known about it, of course, but before the wedding she'd been blinded by love, not to mention the estates and the jet and the jewels. Somehow she'd imagined the will could be changed once she was inside the walls of the castle. It really wasn't fair that Sam hadn't been able to dispose of his vast fortune as he saw fit, that his ungrateful children, who had no sense of style or elegance, should inherit almost everything. The little monsters hadn't been able to wait for their father to keel over, whereas Alysha had gotten him on a serious diet and exercise regimen, which made it seem all the more unfair that he died so soon after they found the Southampton house, or that he should have put so little money down. Her psychic had told her that Sam had at least five more years, at which point the house would've been paid off. Instead, in the middle of a session with the trainer she'd hired, he suffered a massive stroke and passed away twenty-four hours later.

"I just need a little more time, Saul. All will be well." What he didn't know was that she'd already taken out a loan against the art and the furniture, which had kept her going this past year.

"We don't have any more time. If we don't sell something, you could end up losing the co-op as well as the house."

"Then you must convince them, Saul. You're my savior, darling. We will look back on this someday soon and laugh about it, I promise you."

After their dinner at la Grenouille, she invited Billy up to her apartment for coffee, and he seemed every bit as impressed as she'd hoped. The doorman had appeared at just the right moment to help them out of the car, and said, "Welcome home, Contessa." She was almost impressed herself as they stepped directly from the elevator into her foyer, with its black-and-white marble floor and coffered ormolu ceiling. She pointed out the major paintings—the mortgaged Renoirs and the Monet—as they made their way to the living room, where there was no need to point out the view of Central Park. Billy walked over to the windows over Fifth Avenue and whistled. "Now that's what I call a view."

"One gets used to it, after all this time, but I suppose I am very lucky."

"It's really something."

"Come see the rest of the apartment," she said, taking him on a brief tour, which ended in the master bedroom.

"Oh, Billy, you must think I'm terrible," she said, burying her head in his shoulder after crawling up from a longish sojourn between his thighs.

"No, I think you're wonderful," he said.

"I couldn't help myself," she replied.

The next day she gave him a pair of cabochon sapphire cuff links from Cartier.

"I'm . . . speechless," he said after opening the little red box in his suite at the Carlyle. "I don't think anybody has ever given me anything this nice." He looked positively misty-eyed. "They're beautiful. I . . . I can't thank you."

"I'm so glad you like them, darling."

"I love them."

That night he made love like a teenager, and for the first time they stayed together until morning.

Three nights later she again spent the night at his suite. She was already up when the phone rang with his wake-up call.

"Darling," she said, "I can't find my jewels. When I went out to the living room, the door to the suite was wide open."

When they took inventory, it seemed that her earrings and necklace were missing, along with Billy's cuff links and several hundred dollars in cash.

She clutched him and buried her head in his chest. "It's terrifying to think they were right here in the room while we were sleeping."

Billy called the manager and demanded to know what kind of security they had in this goddamned hotel.

"I think their attitude is appalling," Alysha said after their initial interview with the hotel manager and the head of security.

"More worried about covering their asses than solving the crime."

That evening, the head of security knocked on the door and said they were still investigating. "Mr. Laube, can I ask you how long you've known Ms. de Sante?" Outraged, Billy threatened to move out that very night.

"Don't worry," Billy told Alysha later. "Between my insurance company and the hotel's, we'll reimburse you for your jewelry, if you can just give me an appraisal."

"Oh, darling, that's so sweet of you."

"No, it was sweet of you to buy me those cuff links. I'd just like to get my hands on the bastard who swiped them."

"There was a gentleman looking for you earlier," her doorman told her when she arrived home that night. "He wouldn't leave his name. I think he was trying to serve you with some kind of legal document. Of course I told him that you were out of town."

"There must be some mistake," she said, but Saul called the next day to confirm that she should indeed expect a subpoena.

"They're seeking a summary judgment of default and they want to depose you."

"I have no idea what any of that means," she said, "and I told you I just need a little more time."

"You can dodge the summons for a few days or a week, but sooner or later you'll have to give your deposition. And you're going to have to pay off the loan."

"Tell those nasty lawyers I'm far too busy at the moment for their silly deposition." The gala was only three days away, for one thing, and she was on the seating committee, which had to finalize the assignment of tables today, a very delicate operation that involved accommodating the large egos of major donors, separating enemies, and rewarding friends. And she had her final fitting at Valentino.

She instructed her doormen to tell all callers, except for Mr. Laube, that she was in Paris.

The night of the gala, Alysha wore the strapless white lace Valentino with a black bodice. And she had meanwhile taken Billy to Dunhill for a made-to-measure single-breasted tux with peaked lapels. He couldn't quite believe it cost three thousand dollars, but she told him that such a godlike build deserved custom suiting.

Lincoln Center's plaza, framed by the soaring columns of the opera house, Avery Fisher and the New York State Theater, seemed to Alysha a suitable stage for the great occasion. Billy took her arm as they disembarked at the drop-off area and escorted her up the steps. The photographers lining the red carpet began to stir, repeating her name as they readied themselves for her entrance.

They began to snap; then one of them stepped forward. "Alysha de Sante?"

"Yes?"

He handed her a yellow envelope. "You've been served."

"What the hell," Billy said.

Alysha dropped the envelope, but on second thoughts, she realized that she could hardly leave it behind, and so she asked Billy to pick it up for her, the whole scene recorded as the cameras continued to flash, Alysha repairing her smile and leading the bewildered Billy through the gauntlet, turning to see Kip and Mary Trotter, who were right behind them, witnesses to the whole fiasco.

"What was all that about?" Billy asked, blinking and frowning, once they were inside.

"Oh, darling, I didn't want to bore you with my problems," she said in a quavering voice. She realized she had to present her own version of events before he heard any malicious gossip, or, God forbid, read an unflattering account in some column. But first she had to fulfill her role as gala co-chair and escort of the evening's distinguished honoree.

"Whatever it is, it's nothing we can't fix," he said, squeezing her hand. The collective pronoun thrilled her even more than his compassionate expression; it was true—truer than he could possibly imagine—that with his help, her problems would simply vanish. It was all so simple, really. She would bare her soul to him and he would rescue her.

Mary Trotter took her by the elbow. "Anything wrong?"

"Everything is absolutely wonderful," Alysha replied.

And indeed it was. She and Billy circulated through the crowd, accepting compliments. Alysha knew everyone and introduced Billy to those dignitaries with whom he was not yet acquainted, including the director of the ballet and the mayor. At one point when they became separated, she introduced herself to Zach Hunter, the actor, who would be more or less a contemporary of Billy's.

"Very nice to meet you," he said, looking over her shoulder.

"My gentleman friend, Billy Laube, is a big fan of yours," Alysha said. "I know he'd be delighted to meet you."

"Billy Laube? You mean, like, the Laube Foundation?"

She nodded, pointing to Billy, who stood a head above the crowd a few yards away. "Come say hello to Billy."

She led him over and introduced them. Billy seemed relieved to see Alysha and delighted to meet a movie star. It turned out they had a friend in common, someone in Los Angeles named Ray Stark. They engaged in an enthusiastic exchange, much of it relating to the Denver Broncos football team. When they separated to find their respective tables, Alysha said, "Who *was* that man?"

"You didn't recognize Zach Hunter? Are you that young? He's an actor, a movie star. At least he was. I thought you knew him."

"He introduced himself and told me I was the most beautiful woman in the room. I thought perhaps he did look familiar. But then he kept talking to me, so I thought I would introduce him to you so he would know I had a boyfriend."

"Wow," Billy said. "Zac Hunter was hitting on you. And you didn't even know it."

"Perhaps he was a little before my time, or else he is more popular here than in Europe," she said, taking his arm and leading him to the table.

*   *   *

The evening was an unalloyed triumph, and anyone expecting to see Alysha nervous or humbled was disappointed. She took the stage after appetizers and introduced Billy at some length, and he gave a very charming and self-deprecating speech that she had written for him with the help of her Wellesley-educated assistant. The performances were first-rate; even Billy seemed to enjoy the show, which at twenty minutes was just long enough to satisfy the faithful without alienating the banker husbands who had to be at work early the next morning. She knew there was a little buzz concerning the events out on the red carpet, but she chose to rise above it. All that mattered was what Billy thought. The rest of them would follow in his wake.

"You were wonderful," she told him, safely in the car shortly after eleven.

"You're the wonderful one," he said, throwing his big lumberjack arm around her and pulling her close. "I was worried about you."

"You're sweet," she said, "but I don't want you to worry. I'm used to these attacks. They are jealous of me, and they wish to see me suffer, but I won't give them the satisfaction." She buried her head in his shoulder.

"Who? Who's attacking you?"

"The children."

"Children?"

"My late husband's children. They hate me—they want to ruin me. They are contesting the beastly will and they have frozen my assets. My lawyers tell me we will win in the end, but before we do, I may lose my house in

Southampton. Maybe even my apartment. Oh, Billy, I didn't want you to become mixed up in this nasty business."

"Well, it sounds like you need somebody to get mixed up in it. What was the summons all about?"

"It's about the mortgage. They're going to foreclose on my beautiful house."

"Nobody's going to foreclose on anything. Not if I have anything to say about it."

"I can't ask you to rescue me."

"You don't have to ask," he said, pulling her closer.

The next day, Billy canceled his lunch time and walked over to Cartier to look at rings. He'd almost proposed to her last night in the car, but he had old-fashioned ideas about propriety and presentation. He wanted to do it right. He wanted to have the ring and the proper setting for the proposal. Casting his mind about for a place, he realized that Alysha would be the person who would know the perfect location. In the past few weeks he had come more and more to rely on her. He realized that he liked this feeling of surrender, of being taken care of. She seemed to know everyone and everything. All he had to do was show up and be himself. They made a good team.

After fifteen minutes in the store, his head was spinning. Emerald cut, marquise cut, pear and princess . . . color and clarity. And he was shocked by how much you could spend on a fairly modest-looking diamond ring. Billy had little experience with jewelry. Most of the jewelry he'd given his first wife had originally belonged to his mother.

"I'm going on my break," the salesgirl said, "but my colleague will be happy to help you." She indicated a slim young man in a tight black suit, whose hair was combed to a peak in the center of his head.

"Mr. Laube, isn't it?" he said.

Billy nodded, surprised at being recognized by such an unlikely figure.

"Miss de Sante is a client," he said cheerfully. "A very fine lady. A very refined lady, I should say."

Billy nodded, wondering how this odd young fellow knew so much about him.

"I'm sorry you didn't like the cuff links," he said.

"I beg your pardon?"

"The cuff links. That Miss de Sante bought for you. She said they weren't your cup of tea."

"Cuff links? What are you talking about? You mean the sapphire cuff links?"

He nodded. "The ones she returned last week."

"That's impossible," Billy said.

"Perhaps I'm mistaken," the clerk said.

"She returned them?"

"That was my impression."

"This happened . . . recently?"

"Yes, last week."

"Could I see these cuff links?"

"You want to look at them again?" the clerk asked nervously.

"I think I need to see them," Billy said.

The day after the gala, the calls started coming in at eleven. All the girls agreed the night had been a big success. They assured Alysha that she and Billy were the cutest couple in town, and several wanted to know when they could expect an announcement.

When she hadn't heard from Billy by two, she decided to check in. His secretary said he was in a meeting.

"Did you give him my previous message?" she demanded the next time she called, told that he was still unavailable.

"I gave Mr. Laube all of his messages." From the first time they'd spoken, Alysha hadn't liked her attitude, and she vowed to get rid of her, perhaps sooner rather than later.

"If you value your job at all, I strongly suggest that you tell Mr. Laube I'm on the phone."

"I'm sorry, Mr. Laube is unavailable."

This woman was simply intolerable, but Alysha was stymied. At one time, she'd found it charming that Billy was one of the last men on earth subsisting without benefit of a cell phone, but now it was simply infuriating. "Tell Mr. Laube it's urgent that he call me at home immediately."

At eight and again at eight-thirty she called the Carlyle, where the switchboard operator told her that Mr. Laube was not accepting calls.

"I'm his fiancée," Alysha said. "I demand to speak to him."

"I'm sorry, but my instructions were very clear."

"How dare you tell me I can't speak to my fiancé? I demand to speak to the manager."

But the buffoon of a manager was no more cooperative than the switchboard operator, and he seemed unmoved when Alysha told him that she was a very good friend of the owner and would have them both fired.

The next day, his awful secretary told her that Billy was out of town. Two days later, she heard from a friend that he was shooting at an estate in Norfolk. She couldn't understand what had gone wrong. He'd been so loving, so concerned the night of the gala. Someone must have poisoned him against her. Someone had told him something, but what? Of course she knew she had enemies; a girl in her position was naturally a target of jealousy and resentment. Could someone have told him about Riyadh? If she had the opportunity, she would tell him that it wasn't her choice, that she was barely sixteen when her mother had arrived one day at the convent, after an absence of almost a year, and taken her away, promising a great adventure, reminding her about the prince, who'd seen her the previous summer in Monaco.

Billy was still traveling when she sat through her deposition a month later. Her lawyer prevented her from answering most of the questions, but once they were alone, he turned gloomy. "I can stave off a summary judgment for a few weeks at best," he said. "We've got to come up with some kind of plan."

That night, she called Mary Trotter and asked her to dinner the following Thursday, having heard that Mary was giving a party that night for Jake Taplow, the software billionaire.

"I'm so sorry," Mary said, "but I'm afraid we're busy that night."

"Perhaps we could combine our little soirees."

"I don't think so, Alysha."

"Well, you're actually the first couple I've called, so I could easily postpone my dinner and join you that night."

"I don't think you'd feel comfortable, darling." She paused. "Sonja Grossman's coming, and I know how you two feel about each other."

"That's silly. I don't have anything against Sonja." She was more than willing to be magnanimous about her former stepdaughter, if necessary.

"Well, I'm glad to hear it, but Sonja seems to be nursing some silly grudge. I certainly haven't ever discussed it with her, but I think it's safe to say she's not your biggest fan, and I'd hate to subject you to an awkward situation. And the fact is, she's bringing Billy Laube as her date. They met in London and apparently he gave her a ride home on his plane, and, well, honestly, Alysha, I wouldn't dream of putting you in that position. I think it's terrible the way he dropped you; everyone's saying it's practically a breach of promise. It's shameful, but honestly, what can I do? My hands are tied. I had no idea they were an item when I invited Sonja. But let's by all means get together this weekend in Southampton, just the three of us."

The Waiter

"The problem with America," she said, "there is no context. Anyone can tell you anything."

"Exactly."

"You just don't know."

"*You* knew."

"Well, yes, *I* knew. But not until later."

I'd arrived in the middle of a story. Like my country, it seemed, I was lacking context.

"This is Seth," Cara said. The other woman was clearly foreign, possibly Italian; attractive in a windblown, care-less fashion. Not as beautiful as Cara, who made me queasy with desire, but better-looking than I wished she were, since she had pretty much dismissed me at a glance. And her air of entitlement seemed to go beyond what her appearance would have merited. Though she was wearing jeans and a man's oxford shirt, her watch and jewelry probably cost more than my tuition for the next year, with plenty left over for room and board. She made me feel like a bumpkin, and I was already practically paralyzed with insecurity in Cara's presence. Between them, they seemed to present such an unassailable front of sophistication and beauty that I concentrated on the other girl's moles, one on her chin and another above her lip. It seemed to me, in my limited experience, that European women had more growths and marks than American girls did. I tried to hold hers against her, since she was clearly holding something against me. Cara on her own was daunting enough, with her casual aura of boarding school, country clubs and European vacations. I could hardly think of anything or anyone else that summer.

"Marella's just telling me a story."

"It is really not so interesting."

"I like a good story," I said.

"Well, of course," Marella said. "We all like a good story."

"Seth's a writer," Cara said.

She sucked hard on her cigarette and held the smoke in. "How *wonderful*," she said, looking out across the street toward the ocean. "What has he written?"

"I'm a student, actually," I said. "Studying to be a writer."

She was unable to suppress her contempt. "Only in America do they think that they can teach you this thing. To create literature. Do you think Proust studied—what do you call it?—'creative literature'? Or Kafka or Calvino? In Europe we don't believe a professor can teach you to have the soul of an artist. Even the English, they don't think this."

I could see and smell the ocean across the road from the café, and I was suddenly seized by the desire to run down across the beach and jump into the surf and swim far out into the waves. No, actually, that's poeticizing. Trying to be *writerly*. What I was actually seized by was the desire to hold Marella's head under the water while she thrashed and struggled for air. Still, I would've put up with far worse than this to be sitting next to Cara. I'd been insinuating myself into her presence for weeks. And if there was a story, I figured, I might as well hear it.

"We met him at that new place—what's it called?—it's owned by that terrible man who owns the one I like on Madison in the city. He started talking with Julia when I went to the powder room. Well, you know Julia. She would talk to the hat stand if it said hello. I mean, I *adore* her, really, but you *know* how she can be."

Well, of course I didn't know how she could be or even who she was, but that was the point. She wasn't talking to me, but to Cara, barely tolerating my presence. If I wanted to listen, then there wasn't much she could do about it, but she certainly wasn't going to go out of her way to make me feel included.

"I was just telling your friend about the meteor shower tonight," Marella said the man had said when she came back to the table. "It should be well worth staying up for."

"And you have some special place in mind where she can watch the meteors with you?" Marella said with a sneer. (Or so I choose to imagine—I'm sort of partly reporting and partly projecting, based on what she told us that day.)

"Well," he said, "I haven't entirely decided where I'll be watching from."

"You are keeping your options open," she said, "waiting for the best offer?"

"I think life is best viewed," he said, "as a linked series of improvisations."

"Maurice is renting the Condens' guest house for the month," Julia told her.

"I don't think I know them," Marella said.

"Sure you do," Julia said. "You remember, we were at their Memorial Day party on the beach."

Perhaps Marella let this pass, or else she muttered something about there being far too many parties in the season to remember every single one. She must have been softening up a little, because otherwise she would've frozen out the gentleman at the next table at this point. In fact, she'd already told us she thought he was handsome, his complexion suggestive of Latin blood. "Distinguished-looking," she said, his hair flecked with gray at the temples. He had an accent, but as a foreigner herself, she couldn't quite identify it. Of course, she could have just asked, but her innate snobbishness, I suspected, prevented her from being so direct. That was the funny thing to me—a few well-chosen questions could have removed the suspense and ended the story. Americans, at least the kind I grew up with, come right out and ask where you're from and what you do for a living pretty much in that order, but I guess this was too obvious for Marella. She wouldn't want to demonstrate that much interest, or perhaps it was considered rude where she came from. Anyway, Cara seemed fascinated with the story, and anything that interested Cara was sure to interest me.

"He told us he'd just gotten back from Dubai," she said. "Which, of course, is where all the Russian gangsters go to buy Cartier watches for their mistresses and all the

the Saudi princes go for dirty weekends, but he wasn't Russian and he certainly wasn't Saudi. It seemed he might have been traveling for business—he told us thirty percent of the world's cranes were in Dubai. And Julia asked him if he was a bird-watcher, and I didn't understand what she was talking about; I thought it was just, you know, more Julia craziness. And the guy, he says no, not bird cranes, but cranes for construction. And she says, 'Oh,' and I say, 'What are you talking about?' and they explain to me that crane also is a kind of bird. Although it turns out, believe it or not, he really *is* a bird-watcher. He actually goes on holiday to look for birds. Or so he tells us."

"Seth's a bird-watcher," Cara said.

Pleased as I was to hear my name on her lips, it took me a moment to recall the basis for this claim. The first and only time Cara had visited the house I was renting with my buddies, she had picked up the well-thumbed copy of Roger Tory Peterson's edition of *Audubon's Birds of America,* which belonged to the owners of the house, and asked me if I was a bird-watcher. I'd said yes, the basis for this claim being that my parents kept a bird feeder and because I had recently met George Plimpton, who was a big hero of mine, at a cocktail party and he'd told me, apropos of I don't know what, that he was "dead keen" on birds. I thought this sounded like kind of a good Waspy eccentricity to have if you were trying to impress a girl like Cara.

Marella, on the other hand, having zero interest in my hobbies, was determined to finish her story. "We were about to order a bottle of wine, and he asked us if we would mind a suggestion. He called the waiter over; he had this very casual but authoritative—what do you call it?—the way with the hand. You know how some men can't get the attention of the waiter . . ."

"I hate that," Cara said. "You mean *wave*."

"Yes, well, this corrector, he knew how to *wave* to a waiter."

"What's a corrector?" I asked.

"You should know; you're the writer."

"Honestly, Seth. She means *character*."

"Sorry, it took me a minute."

"He told the waiter to bring us a particular bottle of wine, without making too much of a fuss about it. You know, a man should know about wine, but you don't want him to go on and on about it. Some of these American men can be so obsessive on the subject, trying to show off how much they know. Well, our friend, all he said was that the wine was made by a friend of his in Umbria and he thought it would go well with our food— he'd heard us ordering. So then Julia says, 'Oh, so you're Italian.' And he says, well, yes, on his mother's side. And so Julia asks him where in Italy, and after a long pause he names a little town not far from Lucca, which I happen to know because my friends own the place. So I said, 'You must know the Tamborellis,' and he says, 'Only a little,' because he moved when he was young and lived in France. So Julia asks him where in France, and it's the same thing when I ask him if he knows the d'Arbanvilles. He says he knows them, but not well, because he didn't stay there very long, either."

Over the hour they spent sitting next to him, Marella became obsessed with "placing" this guy while Julia flirted. Something about him set off an alarm for her. She must have thought he was some kind of con man, although she didn't say as much. When she said, "My suspicion was alerted," her glance at me made it clear that I hadn't quite passed the sniff test myself.

The way she told it, she was just looking out for her friend Julia, who'd accepted an invitation to a cocktail party the following evening before the main course arrived. By this time he'd joined their table. And it was the main course that eventually betrayed him, or so Marella believed.

"Julia had ordered the fish and it arrived at the table whole, with all the bones. And Julia is looking at this fish; she doesn't quite know where to start, and our friend says, 'Here, allow me.' And he takes the plate, and it's quite amazing; one two three, he has taken out the bones and made two perfect pieces of the fish, like two pages of an open book. Bravo, very nice. Julia was charmed. I am also impressed. But that's when I knew." She paused, a nasty smile of triumph deforming her face.

"Knew what?" Cara said.

"Darling, don't you see? The manners, the wine, the fish. I mean, it's very charming, being able to undress a fish like that. But what kind of a skill is that really? It was like a lightbulb on top of my head. How do you say? An epiphany. I knew who he was."

I looked suitably baffled and Cara shrugged. "Who was he?"

"Darling, he was a waiter."

It took us a moment to register this. I mean, I understood how she had come to the conclusion that the man might have been a waiter at some point in his life, but I couldn't see how it mattered, and, in fact, I was kind of waiting for Cara to say, "So is Seth." Because that's what I was doing in this little summer paradise, waiting tables at the best restaurant in town, collecting orders and tips from people like Cara's parents. I wasn't really a waiter, having already been accepted to grad school back in the city, and I was in the process of becoming, I hoped, a writer, although my father, the foreman of a maintenance crew in a paper mill, still hoped I would come to my senses and go to law school, and that, too, was possible. At that point in my life, almost anything was possible. At any rate, I knew I wasn't going to be a waiter for the rest of my life, and it didn't really occur to me to be insulted until I saw Cara blushing. I started to become embarrassed, whether for her or myself, I'm not quite sure. I mean, she could have made a joke of it. She could have said, "Well, Seth's a waiter, too," and proved her superiority to this silly woman. But the fact that she didn't made me feel that in her eyes I *was* a waiter, that on some level she accepted this woman's judgment about the social order. It was ridiculous. This was America, wasn't it? We weren't Europeans. I knew I was as good as anybody, that my father was every bit as good as her father, if not better. I believed it in theory anyway. But not in my heart, I realized as I watched her blush and felt myself blushing, as well. And I realized something that I'd only intuited up to that point, that there is a class system in America, even if some of us bottom-dwellers didn't realize it.

Somehow, we never got past that moment. Things had changed between us. She had a tennis lesson after lunch, and my shift started at four, and when I called her later, she was always busy and I knew it was no good. At least she didn't come into the restaurant again. I saw her once at the clam shack with some preppy asshole who was doing his best to look proprietary, but at least she had the decency to seem uncomfortable, nodding almost imperceptibly before turning away. I smoked sullenly, tragically—a *poète maudit* at the beach.

The days grew shorter, the nights almost imperceptibly cooler as September approached. On Monday nights, when the restaurant was closed, we had a staff clam bake on the beach, and the following morning I awoke with cotton mouth, my fingers smelling like clams and butter and cigarettes. On the last Monday in August, I finally went home with the hostess, a bouncy nursing major from Stony Brook who'd been flirting with me all summer. I woke up with a nasty hangover at dawn and slipped out while she slept, carrying my shoes across the cold, dewy lawn to my car.

Then, on Labor Day weekend, I saw Cara again at a party. In her sleeveless turquoise blouse and her clam diggers, she looked like someone from a more glamorous era. I ignored her and threw back another Southside, nodding coldly when she came over to say hello.

"I was afraid I wouldn't see you before you went back to school," she said.

"You know where I work." I had meant to sound bitter, but my voice cracked.

"Don't be like that," she said. "Come on."

She took my hand and led me out back to the boathouse and started to kiss me. I realized she was drunk, but

I didn't care. I could smell the sweet alcohol on her breath, along with the stale sea air trapped in the muggy confines of a shack that smelled like the inside of an old sea captain's trunk. Outside, the raspy ocean incessantly pounded the beach. I shoved my tongue in her mouth as she worked her hand down the front of my shorts.

"Fuck me like a waiter," she said.

And so I did.

Penelope on the Pond

Sometimes it helps if I think about all the women in world history who've been in my position, of Anne Boleyn waiting for her Henry, or what's her name waiting for Odysseus to come back from the Trojan War. (I've been reading a lot since I've been here, in case you can't tell, browsing through these paperbacks mildewing on the bookshelves here in the cabin.) Sometimes it feels like I've been here forever. But some mornings I wake up with a dreamy feeling of being outside of time, of being able to wait as long as he needs me to. And I think that's one of the things he loves about me—his own time's so regulated and regimented and subdivided into little pieces, while I can just go with the flow. I try to get him to see that it's all an illusion anyway, that we all have to live in the moment, and not get too attached to outcomes, but for now he has to do what he has to do. It's his karma; I understand. I can wait. This morning I woke up and found myself in that still, gray moment right between night and morning. The sun hadn't showed through the trees yet, but the clearing around the pond was visible and a beaver was carving a V into the silver surface of the water, and I realized this phase of my existence is as fleeting as the beaver's wake.

Now it's almost eleven o'clock and I'm wondering where he is and what he's doing. I mean, I know he's at some grange hall in Iowa, according to the schedule, but I wish I had a constant video feed so I could see him and hear him all day long, like I used to when I was working with him. As for the nights, it doesn't take a genius to figure out what I wish for then. I still can't believe how good it is. How good it was, I should say, since I haven't seen him in almost three weeks.

I should take up knitting or something. What do you call it? Needlepoint. Make him a scarf, or a hat, or a pillow with a slutty slogan. Give me something to do with my hands besides texting him and touching myself. Last night I made myself come four times. I try to keep the texting to a minimum, though, 'cause it's risky. (The touching, on the other hand, is healthy.) And E-mail's out of the question. If I could, I'd send him naked pictures every few hours. But he calls me every day, sometimes more if he can slip away. And sometimes I get to see him on TV. Last week he was on *The View*, and he was so fucking cute, I almost died. I could tell the girls thought so, too, even that Republican blow-up doll Elisabeth Hasselbeck. She was ready to put her ideological differences aside, along with her panties. It's a good thing I'm not the jealous type. I love it when other women think he's hot. They're right: He is. If they only knew.

To clear my mind, I chant and meditate. Sometimes I get frustrated, though, being sidelined like this, not being able to share it with him and help him, or tell him who's totally full of shit and when he's full of shit himself. For three months we were together every day, and it was great. I was on staff as a "media consultant." Of course, we had to be careful. We had separate hotel rooms and all, and PDAs were strictly prohibited, but we still managed to steal time alone together. Like I said, we tried to play it really safe. But once in a while we just couldn't help risking it all—the quickie out behind the restaurant in Des Moines, the blow job in the backseat of the taxi in D.C. I know it's crazy, but when the stakes are that high, the sex is unbelievable. Anybody who's ever been married can tell you what happens to the thrills when there's no risk.

It was one of those love-at-first-sight things. We locked eyes at a restaurant in New York. I thought he was incredibly good-looking and I could tell from the way people were fussing and coming over to his table that he was a big deal, but honestly, I didn't recognize him. Even so, looking into his eyes convinced me. It was only after I'd been picturing him naked for twenty minutes that my girlfriend turned around and said, "Oh my God, don't you know who that is?" What can I say—I don't spend my waking hours glued to C-SPAN, but of course it clicked as soon as she said it. I knew he looked familiar. He was still eating when we walked out, and I couldn't catch his eye, he told me later he'd deliberately not looked over when I was leaving, pretending to be all into what the people he was with were saying, even though he was totally distracted and had no idea. He waited till I was gone and then excused himself, supposedly to go to the men's room.

He caught up with me on the sidewalk a block away from the restaurant. He introduced himself and asked for my number, and I was really happy I hadn't just imagined it—our intense chemical connection, I mean—and an hour later he called me and, what can I say, I agreed to meet him at his hotel room. I mean, sure, it wasn't exactly subtle of me, going straight to his room for our first date, but I figured it might be a little weird for us to be seen sitting all tête-a-tête at the bar downstairs.

Later I couldn't help thinking how me and my girl-friend were supposed to go to Elio's that night, but when we got there, our table wasn't ready and there were about a thousand people crowded around the bar waiting for a table, and my friend said, "Let's try Elaine's; it's only a few blocks up," and I said sure, what the hell, I hadn't been there in a couple of lifetimes. And that's where I met Tom. And later, when he came running after me down Second Avenue, I'd almost jumped in a cab that was waiting right outside—a homeless guy hoping for a tip was holding the door open—but at the last minute I decided to walk, get some air instead. And that's the only reason Tom caught up with me. Otherwise, I would have been long gone in the cab. I heard what sounded like a gunshot up the street, and when I turned around to look, there was Tom.

It's amazing, the connection we have. I think because I was so far outside of his world, I had a perspective on it that he really needed. Obviously, he's incredibly smart, but he's also been living inside this bubble for so long that he can't always see beyond it, and before that he was a small-town boy, which he still is, in a way. As smart and successful as he is, he's never gotten over being the son of a shit-kicking tobacco farmer, feeling like he had to go to the back door of the big house, and people sometimes think he's slow because of his accent, and even though I'm a lot younger, in some ways I'm way more sophisticated. I mean, I've lived in New York and Ibiza and Paris and I've dated actors and artists and rock stars—yeah, I know, big thrill, I'm so cool. The key to Tom is that he's really smart and knowledgeable and he's also, in his own mind, still a boy picking tobacco on his father's farm. It makes him insecure when he's having tea with some fucking aristo- crat, but he also totally uses it. Like, check out his stump speech, where he basically makes it sound like he didn't have shoes till he got to Duke on scholarship.

I remember the Great Man theory from college, which is basically the idea that individuals can change history. But I have my own theory, call it the Little Man theory, which just basically says that if you want to understand any Big Swinging Dick, you just have to figure out who he was when he was a ten-year-old boy. Tom seems pretty honest about how his childhood made him who he is. In his mind, he's still wearing hand-me-down overalls. And I love that about him. But sometimes I worry that he needs constant reassurance as to his lovability and general wonderfulness, and what happens if I'm not there to give it to him?

Practically the first thing we did was jump into bed, and we've been jumping ever since. When I walked in the door of his hotel room, he said, "You're so hot," and I said, "You're so hot," and the next thing I know, we're ripping each other's clothes off. And God, it was good. It was even better the second time, an hour later, because we weren't in such a rush.

Afterward he looked in my eyes and said, "You're amazing," and I said, "You're amazing." I told him he was awake, and he said, "I feel like I'm dreaming, actually," and I said, "No, I mean you're awake in the Buddhist sense. You're aware and you see yourself reflected in other people. You see beauty and the goodness in other people because you have it within yourself. I felt that about you the minute I looked across the restaurant. I could see you were awake. And it was like everybody else in the place wasn't."

It wasn't really like I taught him anything he didn't already know: I just made him more aware of his own powers. Officially, I was listed as a media consultant, but really I was more like his spiritual adviser. Not in any formal sense, and of course he still goes to the Methodist church when he's home, the same one he grew up going to with his parents. But, like, the other day, I quoted him the sutra that says a person who doesn't aim for enlightenment is like a spoiled child who plays obsessively with a toy while the house is burning down around him. And that night he was on CNN, and the sound bite is Tom saying the president is like a child playing with his toys while the house is burning down around him.

I was on staff for almost six months, mostly on the road, before I met his wife, three months before the Iowa primary. She may be a bitch, but she's no dummy. She took one look at me and didn't like what she saw. Even though she doesn't love him, that doesn't mean she wants to look like a fool. And there are the kids to consider. So that was it; I was off the bus. I understood, of course. I didn't like it, but I couldn't really see that he had much choice. If he hadn't loved me, that would have been the end of it; he would have had the perfect excuse to just dump me.

It's no secret now that they're separated; they haven't had a real marriage in years, and even in its heyday they weren't exactly setting the sheets on fire. I mean, this is the kind of southern girl who wore a surgical glove when she finally gave him a hand job. The last time they had sex was during the Clinton administration.

Twenty years ago it wouldn't have been possible to run for president under these circumstances, but I guess we've come a long way since Bill Clinton creamed on Monica's dress. Not that Tom or anybody on his staff thinks that we've come far enough to elect a president who's getting divorced and fucking a younger woman with—well, let's just say a colorful past. We're not living in France, dude. Which is why I'm here, in the cabin on the pond. Well, actually, I'm here because rumors started to spread, and reporters started coming around to my house. There was a story in the *Star* about Tom and an unnamed former female staffer. Lots of innuendo and a claim by an un-named source—true, actually—that we'd been caught in the shower together. Basically it was decided that I better just drop out of sight for a while.

I try not to get attached to any particular outcome, but it's a struggle to stifle my desire. Once Tom's in office, I can come out of hiding and he can get a divorce. If he doesn't get elected, then everything's that much easier, really. Not that we allow ourselves to consider that possibility. Tom wants to be president more than he wants anything in the world, except for maybe me. That's what he said one night, and you won't hear me contradicting him. But it's hard being this far away and knowing that it will be months before we can really be together. Sometimes I get frustrated. Just now I tried to call him, but he's not picking up, so I call Rob, his right-hand guy, who's also not picking up, which is pretty weird.

The cabin belongs to a buddy of his, a big supporter. I don't know why they call it a cabin, because for all its down-home rustic pretensions, it's pretty damn luxe, the kind of place you see on a hillside in Aspen or Telluride, with that sort of Daniel Boone meets Frank Lloyd Wright look. A kind of contempo mission theme inside, with big leather club chairs, Navajo rugs, and lamps made out of antlers, paintings of English setters and ducks in flight on the walls. *Très* macho, but everything a girl could need is here, except for male companionship—a six-burner professional Viking range to boil water, fully equipped gym, spa and sauna, plasma screens in every room. The views are pretty great, taking in a ten-acre pond and, beyond that, a pasture spreading out to the base of a wooded ridge. I've been out walking every day, but yesterday Tom called and told me not to go in the woods 'cause it's deer season. And to wear orange if I take out the garbage or whatever, which I thought was sweet. When I told him I didn't look good in orange, he got all Big Daddy on me. "Alison, this is for your own protection," he said in that voice he sometimes uses to lecture journalists. Any minute I expected to hear him say, *What the American people want is for Alison Poole to start wearing protective orange clothing during deer season.* "I'm kidding," I said. "Joke." Poor Tom was working on about two hours of sleep a night, plus yesterday this fucking political blog called Below the Beltway printed my name: *Who, exactly, is Alison Poole? And why doesn't the Phipps campaign want to talk about her?* Jerk-offs.

After two days of deer season, even yoga can't quite quell the restlessness. I'm getting a little stir-crazy, and I'm down to my last cup of yogurt, so I decide to go into town for groceries. It's almost a mile from the cabin out to the paved road. I have to stop short of the gate, get out, open the padlock and unchain the gate, get back in the car, drive through and lock it all up again. On the front of the gate is a big PRIVATE PROPERTY, NO TRESPASSING sign. A really determined snoop could just climb over the fence and walk down to the cabin, but he'd be trespassing and I could call the local sheriff, who's been instructed by Skeet Jackson, the owner of the property, to keep an eye on me. From the gate, I drive the three miles into town, if that's the word for a grocery store, a post office, a firehouse and a BP station.

I wave to Cassie, the checkout lady at the Piggly Wiggly, who's my new best friend since last week. "Your boyfriend came by looking for you this morning," she says, causing me to crash my shopping cart into a stack of rock-salt bags. For just a second I'm all excited, and then I think, Wait a minute. How does she know who my boyfriend is? If she does, she shouldn't. And why would he be looking for me, when he knows exactly where I am?

"Boyfriend? I don't have a boyfriend," I say, trying to sound nonchalant.

"Pretty girl like you? This fella was awful cute."

"What'd he say?" I ask. "What makes you think he was looking for me?"

"Showed me your picture."

I'm like, "What'd you tell him?"

"I didn't say nothing," she says. "I figured if you wanted him to know where you was, you would of told him. Whatever's going on between you-all, it ain't none of my business."

"Did he tell you his name?"

She shook her head. "Said you was friends. Asked me how to get to the Jackson place."

I say, "You didn't tell him, did you?"

"Like I said," she says, "I don't stick my nose in other people's business. I said I wasn't rightly sure where it was. But I saw him talking to Pete over at the BP. I don't know, like I said, it ain't none of my business, but he seemed awful nice. Whatever he done, I'm sure he's sorry."

"Thanks, sweetie," I say. "I appreciate you covering for me."

"You don't have any reason to be scared of him, do you?"

"No, I don't think so," I say. "Not physically anyway."

"Tell you what. You take my mobile number," she says, scrawling it on an old receipt. "You can call me anytime. If he gives you any trouble, my husband'll straighten him right out. Jake's already got his buck, so now he's just sitting around on his big ol' butt waiting for turkey season."

So I give her a hug and pick up a few groceries and think about who could have followed me here. Back by the freezer case I call Tom, but he's not picking up. Then I call Rob, who says Tom's speaking to a Rotary Club. I fill him in on the situation here. He thinks it might be somebody from one of the other campaigns. If it were one of the tabloids, he says, they would have offered her cash right up front.

"So what am I supposed to do now?" I say.

"Just go back to the cabin," he says. "If you see anybody, call the sheriff. Then call me."

There's nobody waiting at the gate and no cars visible at the cabin when I pull up. I'm putting the groceries away when I look out the kitchen window and see a man in a camel-hair coat standing on the back porch. He jerks his head in my direction after the jar of Ragu smashes on the kitchen tiles. The only thing that saves me from a full-scale myocardial infarction is the fact that I recognize him. He's standing out there, not sure what to do, probably wondering what I'm going to do.

When I catch my breath, I walk over and pull open the sliding glass door. "What the fuck are you doing here?" I say. "This is private property, and if you don't get your ass out of here, I'm calling the sheriff."

"Sorry," he says. "I didn't mean to scare you."

"What did you mean to do?"

"I just wanted to talk."

"I already told you. I've got nothing more to say."

"Yeah, well," he says. "I wanted to see you."

"Okay, here I am. Get a good look, and then I'm calling the sheriff."

"Please," he says, with this pathetic look on his face. "Can I come in?"

"Hell no," I say.

"Well, you come out, then. Just give me five minutes."

"It's freezing," I say. "Just come in."

"Thanks," he says.

I walk out to the great room and plunk myself down in one of the big club chairs with my arms folded across my chest. "What are you doing here?"

"My job?" He shrugs.

"Harassing me is a job?"

"Actually, I'm not entirely sure why I'm here."

"What does that mean?"

"I wanted to see you again. You wouldn't return my calls."

"How'd you find me?"

"I can't tell you that."

"Protecting your sources?"

"We all have our secrets."

"Not me. My life's an open book."

"Which is why you're hiding out in the middle of nowhere?"

"Not hiding. I just needed some time by myself."

"Must get a little lonely down here."

"I was enjoying the solitude. Builds character. You should try it sometime."

"I don't think I'd like it. I'm a people person."

"I can't believe you just said that."

"It was supposed to be funny."

"It was, trust me."

"So?"

"So?"

"This is the part where I ask you if Skeet Jackson's a good friend of yours."

"Why would you ask that?"

"Because according to county records, he owns the place."

"Oh, right," I say. "Skeet's an old friend of the family."

"So he just lent you his house? Help me out here. *Why* did he lend you his house?"

"I told you. I just needed to get away. Do some thinking. A little writing. Skeet offered."

"Awfully generous of him."

"Skeet's a generous guy."

"He's been very generous to Senator Phipps."

"Let's cut the shit," I say. "Why don't you just come out and say what it is you want?"

"I wanted to see you again."

"Right. And I'm here for the deer hunting."

Of course, as soon as I say that, I realize I'm sort of dropping the pretense. We both know why I'm here. I first met Frank about six months ago, when I was working on the campaign, at a party in D.C., although I didn't know he was from Below the Beltway at first; some fucking media consultant I turn out to be. I'd had a couple of cocktails and he asked me where I worked and I'm telling him about the senator, and when he finally gets around to telling me he writes a political blog, I'm worrying that maybe I've said a little too much—that I was a little too free and easy about my closeness to Tom, partly because he was cute and I wanted to impress him at the same time that I wanted to keep him at a distance and remind myself that I was totally taken. All of a sudden he asks flat out if I'm dating Tom, and I say, of course not, so he says, "Well, then, will you come to dinner with me tomorrow night?" So I end up having dinner with him just to throw him off the scent, although it's not like it's such a chore, since he's about as hot as a habanero and Tom's been at the lake house with his family the last four days.

I realize, if I'm not careful, I could get into a sticky situation, so I have the genius idea of telling him that as much as I like him, I'm seeing someone else. When he asks again if it's Tom, I say, "No, it's another staffer, but I can't talk about it." He dropped me off that night at the condo I was borrowing and gave me a semi-innocent kiss good night. The next day he posted something sweet about me being the best-looking girl on any campaign staff, and that was that. Except that he calls me every couple of weeks to chat, and then again last month when the *Star* printed this nasty piece insinuating that Tom was having an affair with an unnamed former staffer whose description fit me like a pair of True Religion jeans. Of course I denied everything, and of course he didn't believe me, and then he asked me if we could get together for a drink. I said I didn't think that would be such a great idea, and after that I stopped taking his calls.

"You drove all the way down here?" I say.

"Except for the last mile or so, which I walked."

"I didn't see your car up at the gate."

"I parked up the road a little, out of sight."

"You're lucky you didn't get shot."

"Folks around here seem friendly enough."

"If I were you, I'd think about hitting the road before it gets dark."

"How about a glass of wine before I go?" he says, taking a bottle out of his backpack. "This is the one you liked so much when we had dinner that night."

It's true, we had an amazingly delicious bottle of wine that night. He hands me the bottle, a 2001 Châteauneuf-du-Pape. "I remember," I say. "The wine of the Popes."

"Also reputed to have aphrodisiac qualities," he says.

"That didn't really pan out for you, did it?"

"Hope springs eternal," he says.

"Although I guess it worked for those old guys. From what I hear, Popes were like the rock stars of their era in terms of pussy. Oh my God, you're actually blushing. That's so sweet."

"Well, I'm a Catholic. I mean, I used to be."

Part of me knows I should get him out of here as soon as possible, but another part of me's dying for company. So we open the wine and I put out a rock-hard wedge of Brie and Carr's water biscuits—it's actually kind of amazing what you can buy these days at the Piggly Wiggly in East Jesus—and he tells me about what's going on with the various campaigns. He tells me about his last girlfriend, who scarred him for life by sleeping not only with his best friend but also with his best friend's wife; then he asks me about my life. I'm telling him about my year at the ashram, pursuing enlightenment and trying not to lust after my guru, when I suddenly think, Wait a minute. He's getting background for his story. I can, like, visualize the blog post: *The former party girl then sought enlightenment at an ashram run by controversial guru Darpak Lalit* . . . "Are you going to write about this?" I say.

"I don't know," he says. "You do realize it looks kind of incriminating, you staying in a big house owned by one of Phipps's best friends and biggest donors. *Are* you having an affair with Phipps?"

"Why don't you ask me if I'm having an affair with Jackson?"

"Sounds like a nondenial to me."

I hear what sounds like a gunshot somewhere in the distance and then my text tone sounds, the first three bars of Gnarls Barkley's "Crazy." I flip open my phone, to find a text from Tom: *Whassup Sugar Plum?*

I don't know why, I'll probably always wonder, but I can't decide whether or not to tell him what's going on. I don't want to worry him. I feel like I could go either way. I can see reasons for both. I stare at the screen until Frank finally says, "Are you okay?"

"I'm fine," I tell him.

I text back: *Blogger found me. Here now.*
Call Sheriff.
That will b big drama/story.
Dont say anything.
I wasnt born yesterday.

It bothers me, him telling me not to say anything. As if I haven't been the soul of discretion for the last year. Frank is looking at me, puzzled. He glances down at his watch.

Get rid of him.
Dont worry.

I decide to turn my phone off. His tone really bugs me.

"I should probably be heading back," Frank says, downing the last of his wine.

"I guess you should," I say. "I can give you a ride out to the gate."

"Thanks," he says.

When I let him off up by the main road he says, "Don't worry, I'm not going to write about this."

"I really appreciate it," I say.

"Call me sometime." He closes the door, climbs over the gate and walks off down the road.

Driving back to the house, I feel kind of bad for Frank. I mean, he doesn't get the story and he doesn't get laid. He turned out to be a pretty decent guy. And I can't help wondering how far Tom would go to keep us out of the papers. Would he still say he wants me more than he wants to be president? Would he screw somebody to protect our secret? Like, for instance, his wife?

When he calls an hour later the wine's wearing off and the sun is setting and I am sinking into a swamp of doubt.

"What happened?" he says. "Did you get rid of him?"

"Sort of," I say.

"What does that mean?"

"He's gone for the moment."

"What did he ask you? Did my name come up? Please tell me you didn't say anything."

"I told him you fucked like a stallion."

"Jesus, Alison."

"Of course I didn't tell him anything."

"Thank God."

His tone is really pissing me off.

"Listen," he says, "I'll call back in five minutes."

But instead it's Rob who calls back and asks me what happened with Frank. "I handled it," I say, and when he insists on details I tell him I'll give those to Tom then hang up.

When Tom finally calls I've had almost an hour to brood.

"Sorry," he says. "We got a call from Fox and I had to run down to the affiliate for a live feed. So what happened with the blogger? Please tell me we don't have a problem here."

If he'd just asked about me, or sounded concerned and sympathetic, the conversation might have gone in a whole different direction. "I don't know," I say. "That depends."

"On what?"

"He wants to come back for dinner."

"What the hell? I hope you told him to go fuck himself."

"I could have, but that would've pretty much guaranteed a highly incriminating post on his blog tomorrow."

"What the hell does he want?"

"I could be wrong, but I think he wants your girlfriend."

"What are you saying?"

"I'm saying I think he wants me more than he wants the story." When he doesn't respond, I go, "Tom?"

"Did he say that?"

"Not exactly."

"What *did* he say exactly?"

"Well, I can't recount the whole goddamn conversation verbatim. But he made it pretty clear he was interested. And he basically kind of indicated that if I wasn't interested in him then he'd take that to mean I was involved with somebody else."

"What do you mean, he *indicated*?"

"I'm summarizing like ten minutes of back and forth. I'm interpreting."

"You told him you were involved with somebody else, right? We agreed that Rob's our cover story."

"He knows Rob's not straight. I mean, come on, Tom."

"What did you say?"

"What do you want me to say?"

"I want you to get rid of him."

"I can do that."

"Does he have anything solid?"

"He claims he has a source for us getting caught in the shower in Manchester."

"Then why doesn't he just go with it?"

"He may."

"You really think he likes you enough to kill the story?"

"It's possible. He wants to come over here and cook dinner for me tonight. What do you want me to do?"

"I don't know, I have to think about this. Let me talk to Rob."

"You're going to talk to Rob about this," I say, incredulous. "I don't want to know what Rob thinks, Tom. I don't *care* what Rob thinks. I want to know what you think. I want to know what you want me to do."

"Shit, Rob's at the door and I'm late for the V.F.W."

"What do you want me to do about Mr. Below the Beltway."

"I don't know. You're going to have to handle this one, honey."

"I don't know what that means."

"It just means you should do whatever you think is best."

"You mean whatever I *have* to do."

"I have tremendous faith in you, darlin'. I love you. I know I can count on you."

Up until that moment, I'm still hoping. But the way he says he knows he can count on me—that tone of voice, that public-speaking inflection he uses in his speeches—it broke my heart. Even the way he said "darlin'" was stage southern. It wasn't an endearment so much as an imitation of an endearment.

"Alison, honey, I gotta get going. I'll call you later."

He was walking out the door. I couldn't help trying to picture that room, even though it would look pretty much like all the other hotel rooms along the campaign trail, like one of the many rooms I snuck into in Franconia or Nashua, in Cedar Falls or Gastonia—those rooms that conveniently seemed to have no personality and no history, with a vinyl-covered ice bucket flanked by two cellophane-wrapped plastic glasses—without ever really wondering too much about all the people who had been there before us, about what had happened in these rooms. Maybe every room deserves its own bronze plaque, if we only knew. I would never see that room at the Hampton Inn in Dubuque, but I couldn't help wondering if he would remember it, out of all the hundreds of hotel rooms that year, as the place where he traded his soulmate for his something he loved more.

Putting Daisy Down

Life was good. It was one of those April mornings when the warmth of the sun on your skin seems miraculous after the deep freeze of winter and you can almost feel the hair on your arms turning golden, the vivid physicality heightened by the lingering trace of a hangover. Bryce was two over par and he'd just hit the green on thirteen with his six iron. The supernaturally verdant fairway was fringed with cheerful yellow forsythia, some of which concealed the ball Tom McGinty had just hooked with his five wood.

Bryce was playing with the big boys—Tom, Bruce Pickwell and Jeff Weiss. That night, at the club dance, they would share a table with their wives, and after dinner Bryce would be officially welcomed as a member of the club, something he'd been working toward for the past two years.

"What the hell?" Tom said, shading his eyes, looking back down the fairway at the cart barreling toward them.

Bruce removed his finger from his nose and crossed his arms over his chest, girding for confrontation. "Looks like—"

"My wife," Bryce said as the cart bounced ever closer, the baked skin on his arms tingling with a sudden chill.

Even from a distance there was something in her posture, and the speed she was traveling, that spelled trouble.

"Carly," Tom said. "To what do we owe the pleasure?"

Ignoring the greeting, she jumped out of the cart and marched over to Bryce, holding a lavender envelope in one hand, the other clutching her swelling belly, just visible beneath her pink warm-up suit. Glaring at him, she held the envelope at arm's length, between thumb and forefinger, until he took it from her. Her stony visage told the story, even if he hadn't recognized the stationery and the handwriting, the ropy loops spelling out his wife's name and their home address.

Without a word, she turned and drove away. The men watched silently until the cart finally disappeared behind the rise of the thirteenth tee, and then resumed their play, Bryce's partners respectfully somber, their fraternal compassion compounded in equal parts of selfish relief and empathetic dread. Their goodwill seemed only to increase as his game fell apart.

"That's a bitch," Jeff said, patting his back, when Bryce missed a three-footer for par on fourteen.

Bryce drove to Julie's apartment on the Upper West Side directly from the course. He was fond of her, and might even have convinced himself he loved her at one point, but she'd just committed an unpardonable offense, and for the first time in months, underneath the anger swelling into rage as he raced down the Henry Hudson Parkway, he felt a welcome sense of moral clarity. His righteousness was only bolstered by the miraculous parking space a few spots down from the entrance to her building on Ninety-sixth

Street. He couldn't believe she would actually write a letter to his wife. Was she out of her mind, he wondered as he held down the buzzer for 4F.

Her voice over the intercom sounded tentative. "Who is it?"

"It's me," he said, his hand clutching the doorknob.

"Come on up," she said in what seemed to him a false singsongy tone, buzzing him in.

Julie could see that her gambit had backfired as soon as she opened the door. He ignored Cocoa, her longhaired dachshund, who swirled affectionately around his ankles.

"How dare you," he said.

She claimed that she'd done it as much for him as for herself, that she knew he wasn't happy with the status quo.

"*I* was perfectly happy with the status quo," he said, no longer needing to maintain the fiction that he was trapped in his marriage and desperate to be with his mistress. He no longer had to pretend that only fear of his wife's unpredictable behavior and compassion for her precarious emotional state kept him from leaving her. Not that Carly couldn't be unpredictable and volatile, but he'd never really intended to leave her. He could see that clearly now. He was about to have a baby with her.

"But you said—"

"I said a lot of shit. I said what you wanted to hear."

It had been more than this, of course; but she had broken the rules, had violated the sanctity of his marriage, and now he wanted to hurt her.

She appealed for compassion and forgiveness, but all her justifications and her tears failed to move him. Her mascara ran, collecting in the little wrinkles and crow's-feet around her eyes, lines that he'd never noticed before. Looking away from her, he was confronted with the evidence of his folly, framed pictures of the two of them—in front of the Rodin Museum in Paris, on the beach in Montauk and in this very apartment standing amid the bronze Buddhas, ceramic dragons, hexagonal shards of quartz and amethyst. Incense was burning in a little bronze urn on the coffee table. Julie was a believer in meditation, pyramids and crystals, whereas Bryce was feeling very Catholic at this moment. With all the zeal of a newly reformed sinner, he rejected her pleas for forgiveness. Strangely, he felt most sorry for Cocoa, who couldn't possibly understand why his old friend was giving him the cold shoulder. He was genuinely moved by the dog's doleful expression.

His confidence and his clarity ebbed as he approached his own driveway. If only Carly were the screaming and crying type, he might be able to imagine an eventual diminution of the crisis. But as it was, he had no idea what to expect.

Daisy greeted him at the door, rubbing her head against his shin. He crouched down and rubbed her head, scratched behind her ears. Daisy thrummed with appreciation and followed him as he reconnoitered the first floor. Carly was sitting in the sunroom, looking out over the back lawn. The fact that she was neither reading nor knitting didn't seem like a good sign.

He knelt down before her, took her hand in his, and laid his head on her rounded belly. "I don't know what to say—except that it's over. I'm so sorry." As he waited for a response, his head on her taut tummy, he felt Daisy massaging herself on his calf.

"This can't go on," she said.

"It's done," he said.

"She's got to go."

"I've taken care of it."

"I can't have this in the house."

"It was never in the—"

"Not in my condition."

Confused now, he looked up at her, at the lips drawn so thin and tight across her face that it was hard to believe they'd ever kissed his, and then followed her gaze down to the floor, to the dead robin on the carpet.

He could hardly contain his relief as he jumped to his feet, ready to deal with this discrete and tangible problem. He'd picked up dozens of dead birds in his long association with Daisy, whom he'd discovered as a kitten in the garbage room of his building on Ninth Street seven or eight years ago, when he was living in his first apartment in the city. It was the work of a moment to pick up the robin by its tail feathers, swing open the French door and fling the thing out into the yard.

Turning back to his wife, he found her regarding him with a distaste bordering on horror. "You picked it up with your bare hands," she said.

"I can wash them."

"I can't believe you picked it up with your bare hands. Don't imagine for a minute you're going to touch me with those hands."

"I was just about to—"

"I can't have this. I simply can't. I won't live with this."

"She's just being a cat."

"It's unsanitary. It's a health risk for the baby."

"After I wash my hands, I'll shampoo the rug."

"That won't help," she sobbed, lifting her hands to her face. "It's not enough."

"What do you want me to do?" he asked.

"It's your cat," she said. "You figure it out." She lifted herself from the couch with that new, slightly labored motion he had noticed of late, an exaggerated series of pushes and lifts whereby she seemed to be anticipating a larger and more pregnant future, cradling her tummy to support it, although in this case the gesture seemed not only protective but also defensive, as if he constituted a possible threat to the fetus.

The guys in his foursome didn't seem surprised by Carly's absence from the club that night, although they eagerly corroborated the alibi.

"You remember that first trimester, honey."

"Kate was puking like a freshman pledge."

"Don't remind me."

"Actually," Bruce's wife said, "I was lucky that way."

"Still," Bruce said, "it wasn't like you felt like going out every night and painting the town."

"Speaking of which," Jeff said, "let's get another round here."

The windows of the master bedroom were dark when he pulled into the driveway. He congratulated himself on his stealth and silence when he stepped into the guest room, which is where he awoke the next morning, on top of the duvet, fully dressed. A baby bird was lying on his chest, Daisy sitting beside him on the bed, the proud huntress.

"Oh shit," he said. He'd almost forgotten this hazard of the suburban springtime—the baby bird menace. Even with arthritis, she could still catch the fledglings. In his muddled state, he couldn't quite separate out the different components of the guilt that was oppressing him—about the affair, about Daisy's murderous habits, about having overindulged the previous night. Had he come on to anyone at the club? No, not really; he was clean on that score.

Bryce flushed the bird down the guest room's toilet, wondering if he hadn't closed the door the night before, or if Carly had opened it that morning. He showered in the guest bath and crept down the hall to their bedroom, where he fortified himself with four Advil and two Zantac, then dressed and girded himself for the inevitable confrontation.

She was sitting at the kitchen table, reading the paper.

"Good morning," he said, sitting down across from her.

She stood up from the table, cradling her belly, and busied herself at the sink.

"You always try to sound bright and chipper when you're hungover. As if that will somehow fool me."

He didn't feel quite bright and chipper enough to think of a response to this. On the other hand, he was happy to keep the focus on the lesser sin of drinking. "Kate and Serena send their love," he said.

"That's ridiculous," she said. "They don't even know me."

"You met them at the Winter Frolic," he said.

"The Winter *Frolic*."

"Well, anyway." It *was* a little weird, how everything at the country club sounded like high school. A few years ago, when he still lived in the city, he would've sneered at the previous night's event. The term *Winter Frolic* would have been a source of mirth. Everything about it would have aroused his urban cynicism.

"And I suppose last night was called the Spring *Fling*."

He was about to refute this charge before realizing he couldn't.

"Rather appropriately for you," she said.

He went to the refrigerator in search of liquids.

It hadn't been his idea to move out of the city. At least not entirely. He'd been happy enough in the one-bedroom on Columbus. But Carly began complaining about the friction of urban life. First it was the dry cleaner's losing her Marc Jacobs top. Then the guy in the wine store who kept hitting on her, which was totally plausible—she was a beautiful woman, after all. Plus the garbage trucks at three in the morning and the homeless guy who followed her in the park. After the planes had crashed into the towers, she'd had nightmares for months. Wasn't that the sequence of events that had led to their finding themselves in the suburbs? The idea had already been raised before that day, inextricably related to the decision to have children. They would have needed to find a bigger place in the city anyway, as she'd pointed out. No, it definitely hadn't been his idea. But he had wanted to alleviate the anxiety and dissatisfaction that seemed to have taken hold of her even before that terrible day in September.

Somehow, three years before, they'd both believed that marriage would be the cure for a malaise they'd never named or spoken about, for the dark moods that descended upon her and the memories of childhood deprivations—most particularly her vanished father. Later, it seemed that graduate school would be just the thing. Moving to the suburbs was, as he saw it, the latest attempt to make her happy. If he hadn't discovered golf, he would have hated it out here, almost an hour from Grand Central. The pleasure he discovered in the game raised his tolerance for certain cultural clichés, although he maintained enough of his urban-hipster sensibility to forswear the kind of brown-and-white footwear that looked like saddle shoes, as well as certain shades of pink and green. And he was probably the only guy at the club with a Celtic cross tattooed on his left shoulder. And what would they think if they knew about Carly's tattoo? Even he had been a little shocked when she first proposed it.

Much as he would have loved to escape to the green refuge of the course that morning, he knew he had to cancel his game. The problem then became how to get through the rest of the day without a confrontation.

Carly went to the stove and returned with a plate, which she dropped on the place mat in front of him. "Your breakfast," she said.

On the plate were two raw eggs, two strips of raw bacon and two pieces of white bread.

A chilly truce prevailed through the afternoon. He trimmed the boxwoods, something he'd been promising to do for two weeks, and later took her to the Barnes & Noble at the mall, where she picked up a book called *Taking Charge of Your Pregnancy.*

That night, they sat in the den together and watched *The Sopranos* and then *The Tudors,* a ritual that suddenly seemed fraught with peril. Carly tended to take her movies and TV shows very personally, to generalize the behavior of individual characters. As a married man, Bryce didn't want to be represented by Tony Soprano and Henry VIII. When Tony had been sleeping with the Russian babe back in season three, Bryce somehow got blamed for Tony's behavior. "You guys are just slaves to your dicks," she said. And, yes, okay, he'd been guilty as charged back then. Fortunately, Tony wasn't screwing anyone this week, although, astonishingly, he killed his nephew Christopher.

"I can't believe he did that," Bryce said. "I mean, how could he do that?"

"He was a hopeless drug addict," Carly said.

"Well, yeah, but still."

"Not to mention a cold-blooded killer."

"I guess."

Bryce was comfortable dealing with the major crimes and mortal sins of others. He tried to remember whether adultery was a mortal sin. *Thou shalt not covet thy neighbor's wife.* It didn't seem like it should be right up there with murder. Carly didn't have much to say about Tony's latest offense, but she pitched a fit when Daisy jumped up on Bryce's lap. "Get her away from me!" Under normal circumstances, Bryce might've stuck up for his cat, but tonight he put her outside without protest.

Shortly after Anne Boleyn professed to be insulted by Henry's offer to make her his one and only royal squeeze, Carly said she was going to the kitchen to get a snack. Bryce said he'd see her upstairs.

He raced through his ablutions in the master bath and managed to slip between the sheets and pick up his book before she ascended the stairs. For a moment, as she paused in the bedroom doorway, he was certain she would challenge his presence there, but when he finally allowed himself to look up from his book, she was standing in front of the mirror, rubbing her belly, and observing her reflected image, as if trying to verify and fathom the great mystery of her condition.

Ten minutes later she climbed ponderously into the bed beside him. "I can't have Daisy dragging mice and birds all through the house in my condition," she said.

"She's a cat," he said. "That's what cats do."

"I can't have it."

"Maybe we can keep her inside for the next few months."

"No," she said. "She has to go."

"Go?"

"I'm having a baby, in case you haven't noticed."

"You want me to give her away? She's been with me for ten years."

"She's had a good life. You said yourself she's getting old. Didn't the vet just tell you she had arthritis?"

"You want me to put her down?" He could hardly believe it. But when he looked over at her, her face had a hard glaze of implacability, with which he was all too familiar.

"I don't think this is too much to ask when I'm carrying your child."

"Maybe I could find a home for her."

"If you can't do this one thing for me, after what you've put me through . . ."

Seeing the tears welling in her eyes, he realized she was serious and he understood that it would not be enough to

find another home for Daisy. "Don't cry," he said, sliding
across the bed to take her in his arms. She tried to pull
away, but eventually she buried her head in his shoulder,
sobbing inconsolably.

He could have tried to find a home for her—that was what
haunted him later. But he was genuinely sorry for his
betrayal and felt bound to honor Carly's wish, cruel and
unnecessary though it seemed to him. This, apparently,
was the price of his transgression.

He postponed it a few days in the hopes that Carly
might soften, but he could feel the tension whenever
Daisy entered the room, and then again at bedtime. After
he found a baby chipmunk in the hallway, he called and
made an appointment for the following day.

He gave his name to Susanna, the vet's receptionist, a
freckled blonde, whose normally bouncy manner was
appropriately subdued on this occasion; it was she who'd
given Bryce the appointment after he'd explained its
purpose.

Despite his previous diagnosis of arthritis, the vet was
somewhat reluctant. "We've been getting good results
with glucosamine," he said. "Unless you think she's been
suffering."

"I really think it would be best," Bryce said.

Given the choice, he opted to stay with Daisy and hold
her to the end. The vet shaved a patch of fur on her foreleg
before injecting her. Bryce would never forget the way she
looked at him as the vet inserted the needle into her vein.
She hissed in protest and tried to squirm out of his grasp,
as if she knew what was about to happen. It was over in

seconds. Daisy relaxed in his arms as the light faded from her eyes. He felt her exhale and then she was suddenly heavier in his arms.

The vet excused himself and told Bryce he'd give him time to regain his composure.

A few minutes later, Susanna came in, opening the door gingerly and tiptoeing forward. "I know how hard it is," she said, placing a hand on his cheek and wiping the tears away. "I went though it myself last year."

That night, Carly made love to him for the first time in weeks. As bad as he felt about Daisy, he believed that he had atoned for his transgression and righted the imbalance between them. After all that had happened, they were tentative and tender with each other, and he woke up the next morning feeling as if they had weathered their crisis. He was certain that with time he would forget about the grim transaction. But in fact, as Carly grew larger with their baby, his sense of injustice and of guilt about his own cowardly acquiescence seemed to intensify. Sometimes when they were watching television and she would rub his hand over her belly he would wonder why he couldn't have found a home for Daisy, why Carly'd been so brutal as to close off that option. What kind of a person was he married to? Hell, he could have asked Julie to take the cat. His anger toward her had faded in recent weeks, and he had to resist the urge to call.

For years, even before she was pregnant and had the excuse of hormones, Bryce had lived in fear of his wife's dark moods, but now he found himself losing patience with her complaints and her piques. "Jesus Christ, you'd think you were the first person to have a baby," he snapped one day after she moaned yet again about her swollen ankles.

He waited until after the baby was born to call Susanna, from the vet's office, who'd given him her number that day.

The Debutante's Return

The call came at six in the morning, as she was returning home from a party that had lasted far too long, if no longer than several others she'd recently attended. This one had started at a nightclub on Fourteenth Street and ended on a rooftop in SoHo. She counted ten rings while she was fumbling with the locks on her apartment door, and another two before she reached the bedroom. Messed up as she was, she had a pretty clear idea of what the call would be about.

"You best come home," Martha said. "You mama done had another stroke."

She didn't remember the rest of the conversation. She was sitting on the bed with the telephone cradled in her lap when a strange man appeared in the doorway. "Nice place," he said. "You got any vodka?" Apparently, she'd brought him home with her. He was wearing a pearl-gray fedora and a white silk scarf. She was surprised to find herself with a man in a fedora, and even more surprised at the sudden impulse to tell him not to wear it indoors.

She led him to the kitchen, opened the freezer, and handed him the frosty bottle of Absolut. "Take it," she said, maneuvering him out into the hallway. Before he quite knew what was happening, she'd pulled the front door shut and locked him out.

Somehow, this time, she knew the party was over, that she was finished with all that. But she had second thoughts when she arrived that afternoon at the Nashville airport, where everyone seemed fatter and slower and the air was shockingly sultry with humidity. Stepping off the plane was like being enveloped in a steaming-hot towel. She remembered once again why she'd fled north in the first place.

She looked frailer than ever in the hospital bed, with onion-paper skin and protruding bones. One side of her face seemed to be frozen. "I'm here, Momma," Faye said when her mother's translucent eyelids fluttered open.

"Bunny, it's you."

"It's me, Momma."

"You look tired. Where's your father?"

"Daddy's not here, Momma. You're in the hospital."

"The hospital? But won't he be worried?"

"We're all worried about you. You gave us a scare. Now get yourself better so we can take you home."

"Who's feeding Bugsy?"

It took Faye a moment to recall Bugsy, a wheaten terrier run over when she was four.

"Martha's taking care of everything back home."

She moved back into her room in the so-called New House, a Tudor pile her grandfather had built in the twenties after subdividing the old family property. The old house, aka the Big House, completed a few years before the Union army took over the city and dispossessed her great-great-grandparents, was now a museum. Its replacement, Faye's childhood home, had once stood in splendid isolation on a sea of bluegrass, but in recent years the suburbs had engulfed the property, now a mere five acres, with ranch houses and split-levels. Her brother was all in favor of selling it, but their mother insisted on staying put, and Faye had strenuously defended her position, yet given this new turn of events, she didn't know that she could hold him off much longer. In fact, it soon became clear that he'd already begun taking the place apart.

Martha catalogued the missing pieces. "Mr. Jimmy come in with a U-Haul last night and took away three carpets, a chifforobe, the dining room table and all the chairs. He say Miss Jordan ain't gonna be givin' no dinner parties nohow."

Faye was glad she'd already decided to stay, knowing it would take all of her strength to protect her mother and to keep her brother at bay. They'd already had the nursing home discussion, and Faye adamantly refused to see her mother shut away like that. Her memory might be failing, but she had Martha to take care of her, and it wasn't as if they lacked the resources to keep the house running. While she sensed this debate would now turn ugly, Faye was determined. She realized her position was more than a little ironic, since more than once she'd expressed the wish that the stupid house, with all its bad plumbing and bourbon fumes and family secrets, would burn to the ground so they could all just get on with their lives. Here in the self-proclaimed Athens of the South, she hated all the nostalgia mongering, the pedigree parsing, and thé casual racism of her brother and his friends. She'd gone to college in Massachusetts, which her grandfather derided as "the Yankiest state in the Union," and then had moved beyond the pale to New York. She returned from time to time, but she'd truly believed when she left at eighteen that she was leaving for good. All of which saddened and mystified her mother, who was, to no small extent, the focus of Faye's apostasy.

Sybil Hayes Teasdale was everything the South expected its daughters to be, and everything that Faye wished to escape. She wore white gloves whenever she left the house, and on those rare occasions when she could be persuaded to speak ill of others, the worst curse she could muster was "common." The Hayes family had achieved prominence in South Carolina before Sybil's grandfather decamped to the more fertile cotton land of the Mississippi Delta, where he made and lost several fortunes and served two terms in the Senate. Her father attended Vanderbilt long enough to acquire a suitable bride, Dottie Trammel, whom he carried back to the Delta plantation. Sybil's most vivid childhood memories centered around the flood of '27, when she and her mother spent two days atop a levee outside of Greenville, waiting to be rescued. Eventually they were picked up in a rowboat and carried to safety. But her father, who stayed behind to help coordinate relief efforts, drowned trying to save one of his men, or so the story was told. Dottie took her daughter and moved in with her parents in Nashville, and while the Trammels always honored the heroic memory of their son-in-law, there was an almost palpable sense of relief that their daughter had returned to civilization.

Her father's death could only have exacerbated that innate southern consciousness of loss and nostalgia, while her mother's family, whose respect for the proprieties was profound, raised her with an exaggerated sense of the perils beyond the family threshold, as if she herself were in imminent danger of being sucked under by muddy torrents. Later, as she started to blossom, this peril was identified as male lasciviousness; she was sent to a finishing school in Switzerland. Returning to Nashville at the age of eighteen, she became the object of intense competition among the eligible men of her generation, who vied to be named one of the six escorts at her debutante ball, held the following spring at the Belle Meade Country Club. Faye's father was not among the chosen, the Teasdales having fallen out with the Trammels over a failed business venture—but he spent the next three years wooing Sybil. Theirs was a storied romance, the beauty with the tragic past and the scion of one of the town's great families, and they were inseparable for the forty-five years of their marriage, although Faye remembered her father as something of a tyrant when it came to his demure and fragile spouse. She'd loved him wholly but was glad she was his daughter, rather than his wife. Even with a staff of six at his disposal, Hunt had demanded constant attention and service from Sybil, and he'd seemed always to be pounding the table and raging against some perceived shortcoming on her part.

Faye had come away from her childhood less than impressed with the institution of marriage. These feelings were reinforced as the sixties gave way to the seventies and their minister at St. George's began railing against free love and women's lib, both of which sounded pretty appealing to teenaged Faye.

Sybil never seemed to feel her oppression as acutely as Faye thought she should, so instead of blaming her father,

Faye blamed his wife for her slavish adoration, adding this sin to the tally of grievances against her mother, along with the injunction against blue jeans, and her constant endorsement of "ladylike" behavior. She would have liked to dismiss her mother as a hopeless prude, but on several occasions she had surprised her parents in the act. Saturday afternoons, after her father's golf game, were consecrated to conjugal sport; Faye and the staff were strictly forbidden to enter the master wing between two and four, and her mother inevitably emerged from her "nap" all glowing and kittenish.

After Hunt collapsed on the fourteenth hole at Belle Meade in the middle of one of his famous tantrums, Sybil seemed to shrink and fade. Faye had come home for the funeral and stayed as long as she could bear it. Though she knew she should feel greater sympathy for her mother and greater grief for her father, at that time all she could think about was getting back to her life in New York. But in the intervening years something within her had changed. Maybe she was simply tired of running. Or maybe her mother's helplessness, along with her brother's eagerness to stick her in a nursing home, had finally awakened her sense of filial duty.

When her brother arrived with the U-Haul that evening, she saw the car and trailer from her room upstairs and went down to confront him. He was in the entry hall with Walter, his longtime yardman, and they were examining the grandfather clock in the entry hall. He looked up, surprised, not having heard her descend the carpeted stairway. "Sis, you scared the shit out of me. Whatever brings you here?"

"Mainly the fact that Momma had a stroke."

"It's a damn shame is what it is," he said. "But I can't say it's a surprise. I saw this coming a mile away. She's been failing for the past year. I talked to the doctor this morning and he says she needs full-time care." Faye had forgotten how much she disliked his voice, the lazy pace and occasional crackerisms. Neither of their parents had ever spoken like that. But despite the trips to Europe and four years at a boarding school in Connecticut, Jimmy had somehow managed to become a good old boy, the kind of guy who attended cockfights and tossed the *N* word around. Perhaps that was his way of rebelling against his heritage and upbringing.

"Well, I'm here now. And she's got Martha."

"Well, sure, but what happens when you skip back to New York? I'm talking about professional care. What she needs is a real facility."

"I'm not skipping back to New York. And Momma doesn't want to go to a home. She's already got one."

"You're going to take care of her? Come on, now, sis. When did you get so damn interested? I can't even remember the last time you visited."

"It was last Christmas, actually."

"Well, we're deeply honored to have you back."

"What are you doing with the clock?"

"Just going to have it fixed. Damn thing hasn't worked right in years."

She watched as they wrestled the clock out the front door, feeling paralyzed and impotent, as if stuck in one of those dreams where speech wouldn't come. After all these years, she was still intimidated by her brother. He was twelve years older and had always treated her like a child, with a mixture of sarcasm and condescension. He had once, when Faye was seven, stuffed her beloved cat Twinkie in the dryer and turned it on, forcing her to watch as the terrified cat tumbled through what seemed to her like a hundred revolutions, until her screams finally brought Martha to the rescue. She watched now as the car rolled away down the long gravel drive, furious with herself for letting him steal the clock.

Over the years in New York, Faye spoke with her mother weekly and even more often with Martha, the housekeeper who had lived with the family for more than forty years and who had originally served as Faye's nanny. Sybil, she'd said, was living increasingly in the past, even before this latest stroke. The physical effects were blessedly minimal; she retained most of her mobility and speech. The doctors were less certain about her mental processes, though reluctant to speculate.

"But there's no reason we can't take care of her at home, is there?"

"She needs to be watched pretty closely," Dr. Cheek said. "I'd recommend hiring a nurse, at least for the first few weeks. But at this time I see no need for institutional care."

"I'd be happy to stop by and check up on her," the younger, good-looking doctor said. He seemed to be flirting, but she had to remind herself that this wasn't New York, that the mean temperature of normal social interactions was much warmer here. Quite possibly, Dr. Harrington was simply demonstrating the dedication and concern appropriate to his profession. Faye was so used to deriding the ritual politesse her mother so cherished, she had to remind herself good manners weren't necessarily insincere.

"Where are we going?" her mother asked for the third time as they pulled off the interstate.

"We're going home, Momma."

"As soon as we get there, I want you to march up to your room and change out of those horrible dungarees. You look as if you're reporting for work on a road crew."

"They're called jeans."

"I know what they are. And they're not appropriate attire for a young lady."

"It's the eighties, Momma."

"I don't want your father to see you in that outfit."

Faye said nothing. She had decided to wait till they were settled in to address this subject.

But when they arrived home, Sybil wanted to see her roses. She seemed utterly lucid. "What's happened to the clock?" she said as soon as they walked in.

"Jimmy's taken it to be fixed."

"It hasn't worked in twenty-seven years," she said. "Why should he fix it right now?"

Her denuded dining room, meanwhile, was concealed behind pocket doors. Faye walked with her up to the master bedroom, which she hadn't entered in years. Everything was more or less as she remembered it from her childhood—the hand-painted wallpaper from Switzerland that offered up a series of fantastical Chinese vistas; the king-size bed with its upholstered headboard, the feather mattress and box spring ordered specially from the same firm that supplied

Claridge's, which Hunt claimed had the most comfortable mattresses in the world; the white vanity where her mother had attempted to teach her the rudiments of makeup. On the other side of the room was her father's dressing table, with monogrammed leather stud boxes, a sterling cigarette lighter, an ivory comb, a tortoise-shell cigarette case, a souvenir ashtray from Augusta National, seven golf trophies and a small gallery of framed family photos. The silver was all bright and polished, as it had been during his lifetime. She wondered if the pearl-handled revolver was still in the top drawer.

"It's so nice to have you home," Sybil said.

"It's nice to be here."

"Have you been making friends at school?"

"More friends than I know what to do with."

"You can never have too many friends, Faye."

"Why don't you rest, Momma. I'll call you for dinner."

Sybil reached out and took her hand.

"I know your brother wants to put me in a home," she said.

To Faye, it seemed remarkable that her mother could have returned so rapidly to the present. "Don't worry. Nobody's going to put you in a home as long as I'm here."

"You know the Yankees, when they invaded, put your great-great-grandmother Eliza out of her home."

"I know, Momma."

"For five years she and your great-great-granddaddy Isaac had to live over a dry-goods store on Broadway while the Yankee officers slept in her bed and spit tobacco juice on her rugs. She died of a broken heart in those rooms over the dry-goods store."

No matter how many times Faye had heard this story, she'd never been certain what a dry-goods store was, or its significance in the story. Would it have been worse if it had been, say, a hardware store?

Sybil didn't mention her husband again until the following evening when Martha called her to dinner in the breakfast room.

"We can't sit down till Hunt comes home," she said. She was perched in her favorite armchair in the sunroom, looking out across the lawn, beyond which the orange Mediterranean roof tiles of a gated community called Tuscan Acres rose over the privet hedge.

Faye sat down across from her and took her hand, which was almost translucent, and freckled with age spots in spite of the white gloves she wore so often. "Daddy's not with us anymore, Momma. He passed away three years ago."

It was as if this was the first time she'd heard the news; tears welled in her eyes and her face contorted with grief.

Faye squeezed her hand as hard as she dared. "Don't you remember, Momma?"

She shook her head, the tears now rolling down her cheeks.

Faye had not been present when her mother learned of her husband's death, and she was witnessing now what she'd missed then. Her grief seemed utterly fresh and unbounded. She appeared to be almost literally melting, slumping lower and lower as the tears poured down her face, a woman devastated by loss. It was almost unbearable to watch.

"What will I do without him?" she finally managed to say.

"You've been doing without him for a while now, Momma."

This scene repeated itself twice more over the course of that week, and each time Sybil was inconsolable. Faye finally decided just to say that Hunt was on a business trip. In fact, she herself had started tearing up whenever she broached the subject of her father's death.

Dr. Harrington came by, as promised, dressed for tennis. If his legs were any indication, Faye imagined he was very fast on the court. He appeared to be in his mid-thirties, roughly her own age. He spent a good fifteen minutes with Sybil and then sat down with Faye in the library.

"Great room," he said, admiring the leather-bound volumes and the hunting prints. Faye had always found it oppressively masculine and studiously old-world.

"How does she seem to you?"

"She seems to be improving."

"She forgets things," Faye said.

"That's understandable."

"For example, that her husband is dead."

"It could be vascular dementia from the stroke, which may reverse itself. I think we also have to consider the possibility of Alzheimer's. I gave her a mini-cog—that's a little test where you ask the patient to remember a list of common household objects and draw the face of a clock. She drew the clock, but she couldn't remember the objects. There's a chance she may improve, but it's more likely we're dealing with progressive dementia. I wish I could be more optimistic. On the other hand, I can say with certainty that she's better off here at home, as long as she's properly cared for. Forgive me for prying, but I gather you live in New York."

She was reminded that there were no secrets here, and for a fleeting moment she was tempted to revise her plan and book the first flight back to New York. "I'll be here for as long as she needs me."

"That could be a long time," he said.

"I know."

"Well, I'm sure your mother is very happy to have you back," he said. "Although I imagine there may be some weeping and gnashing of teeth up in New York."

"I think they're thoroughly sick of me. I stayed too long at the party."

"I doubt that very much."

"There're a few boys up there in New York who wish I'd never left Nashville."

"Way I hear it, there're a few boys down here who wish the same thing."

Now she knew he was flirting, but she wasn't really in the mood. Just now she felt like she'd dated enough men for the next five or six lifetimes.

Over the course of the following week, Sybil inquired repeatedly as to the whereabouts of her husband, and the business trip story was wearing thin. Faye's next idea was to tape Hunt's obituary to her mother's bathroom mirror, hoping that the shock of seeing it there every morning might be partly alleviated by seeing her husband's accomplishments enumerated and praised. But the first morning, Martha came down from Sybil's bedroom to report that she was sobbing uncontrollably in her bed.

"I don't know what I'm going to do without him," she wailed when Faye went up to comfort her.

"He was the only man I ever loved."

"There wasn't another like him," Faye said.

"You know, it was your father who fixed things when the colored people demonstrated at the lunch counters. He was president of the chamber of commerce and he convinced everyone that the time had come to integrate. The only reason so many went along with it was the respect they bore for your father's opinion. He said it was just good business."

The memory of her husband's civic heroism seemed to revive her spirits, and with Faye's help she dressed, then spent the afternoon tending her roses. That night they watched several episodes of *Upstairs, Downstairs* on video. But the next morning, Faye found her crouched on the bathroom floor, weeping. During the night she'd forgotten again, and the sight of the obituary had come as a shock. She spent the rest of the day in bed. Two days later, Faye removed the newspaper clipping from the mirror, and when Sybil asked about Hunt, Faye or Martha would reply that he was away on business, an answer that now seemed to satisfy her.

When Dr. Harrington came by a week after his first visit, Faye declined his invitation to dinner, suggesting instead that he join her for whatever Martha, an excellent cook, was rustling up. The dinner, chicken and egg bread with white gravy and collards, was a guilty pleasure, but the conversation seemed to flag whenever they veered off medical topics, and Dr. Harrington tended to chew with his mouth open, a memory that put her off the idea of kissing him at the door.

When Faye returned from the gym the next morning, she found Martha in a state of agitation. "Mr. Jimmy come by," she said. "He tried to get your momma to sign a power of attorney. She's terrible upset. He try to sweet-talk her first, but she told him she wouldn't sign and he told her she was a foolish old woman and worse." Faye was ahead of her on the stairs, racing for Sybil's bedroom. "She say she don't want to sell her house and she don't want to go to no nursin' home. So Mr Jimmy storm out and your momma, she's in a state."

Sybil was a tiny dark figure in a great sea of linens, sitting upright against the headboard, her hands clenched on her thighs.

"I won't move to Broadway," she said. "I don't care what he says. He can tie a stick of dynamite to me like he did with that stray dog, but I won't sign that paper and I won't move to Broadway."

The next morning, a Saturday, Faye drove over to her brother's house, a sprawling ranch in a gated community called Elysian Hills, and rang his buzzer.

He came to the door wearing a shooting vest over a flannel shirt, his pink scalp glistening through the furrows of his brushed-back hair. "Sis, I was just about to call you. Come on in."

"I don't want to come in. I just want to say don't you dare come round and bully Momma like that again. You can say what you want, but I'm not letting you lock her away. And I'm not letting you loot the house."

He was taken off guard by this last remark; his face, always ruddy, turned a deeper shade of red. "You've really turned into a prime New York bitch, haven't you?"

"It's taken years, but I'm slowly getting there. I didn't say anything when you took Daddy's guns and his watch collection."

"What the hell good were they to you?"

"I could have sold them just as easily as you did."

"I've been taking care of Momma and that house for years while you were off gallivanting around New York with the beautiful people. Hell, I've even been paying your goddamn credit-card bills. Your Chanel and your '21' Club."

"The estate pays my bills. And God knows what else the estate's been paying for. But if you persist in trying to lock Momma up, I'm going to send in a battalion of accountants and lawyers and it's all going to come out in the open. *New York* accountants and lawyers."

That night, Faye went through the family photo albums and found herself revising her memories, as if her childhood were an undervalued asset, like an anonymous painting suddenly revealed to be the work of a master. The cumulative impact of so many smiling faces was impressive. The pleasure her parents so visibly displayed in each other's company seemed to contradict her grim recollections. Looking through hundreds of travel snapshots reminded her of just how many trips they'd taken when she was younger. Jimmy, having gone off to college and marriage, was largely absent from the later pictures, while Faye looked remarkably happy, until she started to develop a pout around the age of thirteen, a sulky expression that said, *I can't believe I have to be here in Europe with my parents when I could be home with my friends.* The picture that eventually made her cry was at first a mystery, a blurry shot of what appeared to be a mermaid in a Venice canal. The woman, a Botticellian blonde in a blue bikini top, seemed to be sitting or lying on a submerged stone step or platform. Below the waist, just visible within the murky water, was a blue-green fish tail. Faye had been in a mermaid period then, sometime around her eighth birthday, and this had been the highlight of her trip. Years later, she learned that her father had staged the tableau. She had long ago forgotten the incident, which along with so much else suggested she had been the happy, spoiled child of loving parents.

After finishing the better part of a bottle of Campari, she called Cal, a former boyfriend, to whom she hadn't spoken in months.

"Was I so awful?" she asked. "Was I just a total screaming bitch?"

"You were wonderful," he said. "The girl of my dreams."

"But you said yourself I broke your heart."

"You couldn't have broken my heart if you hadn't been so damn lovable."

"How could I be so wrong about everything?"

"Not everything," he said.

The next day she had dinner with Dr. Harrington at the club, and made a conscious decision to mute the critical inner voice that had found him wanting the last time out. She soon found herself telling him about her father, stories that she had told before, but never in such a fond fashion, his former flaws transformed now into lovable eccentricities. "He hated being alone," she said, looking away as the doctor masticated his steak. "He used to insist that my mother and I watch television with him, shouting for us to come down-stairs and sit with him. He always seemed to be shouting and cussing, but now it seems funny to me somehow."

When he was driving her home after dinner, an ambulance flashed past with its siren screaming, and when they turned in, three Belle Meade police cars were parked in the driveway.

Faye panicked at the sight of the pulsing blue lights and the metallic, staccato walkie-talkie voices. "Oh my God."

"Let's not jump to any conclusions," Dr. Harrington said.

Not jump to any conclusions? She would have liked to have had the leisure to stay and ask him if he was fucking crazy, but instead she bolted out of the car and ran up the driveway to accost the nearest cop. "Please tell me what's going on. I'm Faye Teasdale."

"There's been an accident, Miss Teasdale," he said, taking hold of her forearm.

"Oh good Christ! Is my mother all right?"

"Your mother's fine. I mean she's not hurt. It's your brother. It seems your mother mistook him for an intruder."

"Where is she?" Without waiting for an answer, Faye rushed up the steps and through the open door, brushing past two more policemen in the hallway. Upstairs, she found her mother in bed, attended by Martha.

Sybil was sipping from a glass. She seemed remarkably calm under the circumstances, far more composed than her daughter.

"Momma, are you all right?"

"I'm fine, Bunny," she said, returning Faye's embrace.

"You didn't know," Faye said hopefully. "You thought it was a burglar."

"It was a burglar all right. He was walking off with the silver."

"She got Mr. Hunt's little pearl-handled Colt from the bedside table," Martha said.

"Your father used to take me to the shooting range on Sundays after church. I heard a noise downstairs, and I knew you were out."

Faye suddenly realized that she hadn't even inquired about her brother's condition. "Is he going to—"

"He gonna be all right. Your momma done shot him in the butt."

"Gave me a mighty big target," Sybil said.

"You couldn't tell who it was in the dark. Could you, Momma?"

"You know those damn Yankees turned Eliza Teasdale out of her own house."

Martha and Faye exchanged a look. "She confused," Martha said.

Sybil shook her head. "Jimmy says I'm losing my mind, but I'll tell you one thing. I can still recognize my own son. And I can recognize a thief."

"Momma, what are you saying?"

She looked up at Faye and stroked her hand. Her gaze was clear and direct. For the first time in weeks, she seemed fully present.

"Did I just say something?" she said. "Don't mind me. I'm a crazy old woman. My mind plays tricks on me. Just ask your brother. He'll be glad to tell you."

The Last Bachelor

Emerging from the surf, Ginny was amazed to discover A.G. sitting cross-legged on her towel, chatting up her niece. Her first reaction was entirely self-conscious—wondering how she looked dripping wet in her ratty blue Speedo—her first impulse to flee. She hadn't seen him in—what, a couple of years? That night after the Alzheimer's ball, when he'd drunkenly asked her to go with him to Saint Barts. After a quick inventory of her own imperfections, she noticed his paunch. When had that happened? Watching him hit on her niece, interpreting the casual slouch of his posture as he leaned on his elbow, she decided that what was interesting wasn't the belly per se but his lack of self-consciousness, that he'd probably never stoop to suck it in or even count it against himself when he was tabulating his own defects. He still had the same boyish, timeless shock of blond hair—she was quite sure he'd taken it very much to heart when she told him, early on, that he looked like Robert Redford. She could read, even from this distance, the old sense of entitlement, the ease and confidence as he turned his charms on a beautiful young woman half his age. This is what had always, in her mind, saved him from being a caricature, that he deviated just enough from the type—even if it was only a question of scale. In this case, the way that his vanity was larger and more impregnable than that of other middle-aged men who obsessively chased younger women, spent hours at the gym, or, failing that, risked herniation trying to, at crucial moments of presentation, inhale that extra flesh around their middles. Perhaps she was reading too much into what could be a simple, innocent tableau, but that, too, was A.G.—the fact that he inspired this kind of hermeneutics. This speculation on Ginny's part was the work of an instant, the interval between two waves breaking around her ankles. Before the second had retreated beneath her feet, she felt angry at herself for the intricacy of her speculation, for caring that much. Wasn't it far more likely that he *was* a type, and that the supposed complexity was her own embroidery on a standard pattern? Hadn't he disappointed even the modest hopes she'd invested in him?

She had reason to chastise herself again, approaching them, when she realized that she was the one sucking in her own stomach, but this was mitigated by the pleasure of seeing his reaction when she sat down beside him and shook the salty water from her hair.

"A.G., this *is* a surprise. I see you've met my niece."

For a man who prided himself on his composure, he was comically discomfited, though he made a valiant recovery, kissing her on the cheek, doing his best to convey the impression that he'd practically been expecting her at any moment. He then excused himself as quickly as one with his exquisite manners could. Ginny had the satisfaction of watching him retreat down the beach, slightly duck-footed as he struggled for purchase in the dry sand. Yes, she remembered that, chasing after him one day through the snow in Aspen—seeing his splayed tracks, thinking it made him even more endearing.

"What was that all about?" she asked Lana, who blushed. It was reassuring somehow, that young women still knew how to blush.

"I don't know. He was like, you know. He was just kind of . . ." She shrugged.

Well, actually, yes, Ginny did know. But she wasn't feeling entirely collegial toward her niece at this moment, appraising her as she imagined A.G. had, and she conjured a strange conceit—that the concavity of a young woman's tummy was precisely calibrated to the paucity of her wisdom. God, she was young. Of course Ginny had watched A.G. pick up women who were no older than her niece. But until this moment she would never have thought of her niece—her little Lana—as having anything in common with those girls. "Kind of what?"

"Well, you know. Friendly."

"You mean he was hitting on you."

"Well, he just kind of sat down. Actually, he walked past me a little and then came back and introduced himself. He asked me if this was Gibson's Beach, and I told him I wasn't from here, and then we just started talking."

"Did he ask you out?"

"Well, he said he was kind of busy this coming week but he'd call me next Monday."

Ginny nodded. She told herself it wasn't Lana's fault. She counted to ten. She tried to tell herself she took no pleasure in this, in feeling, suddenly, so very worldly-wise. "I expect he *is* fairly busy," she said, shaking a cigarette from the pack. "Unless I'm very much mistaken, he's getting married this weekend."

Approaching the house on Gin Lane, the so-called cottage with its sprawling wings, white porches and shingled gray gables, A.G. saw the white tent rising up above the perfectly squared green privet battlements that surrounded the property of his future in-laws. The gates were open. As he drove in, he was presented with a scene of furious activity. He stopped the car in the middle of the driveway and watched. Painters and window washers on ladders had stormed the big house. Three maids waddled like white ducks up the path to the guest house, bearing linens. Half a dozen young men who looked like camp counselors were setting up the tables beneath the tent. Gardeners were scattered about the property, planting and deadheading flowers; still more flowers were coming out of a van from a Manhattan florist. And an anonymous tradesman was taking a leak against the side of the pool house. All of this had been set in motion by his proposal to Pandora Bright Caldwell Keirstead, of Chattanooga, Palm Beach and Southampton, several months before. It wasn't exactly a spur-of-the-moment decision. He'd actually purchased the ring at Graff more than a month before and carried it with him on two dates with Pandy, somehow losing his resolution each time. Finally, he'd invited her to One if by Land, which practically forced his hand, it being notorious as a setting for proposals. Before their appetizers had arrived, two other swains had dropped to their knees in front of their dates. Pandy blushed deeply the first time; the second proposal she pretended not to notice. If she was disappointed that A.G. had stayed seated when he popped the question, she wasn't about to show it.

The announcement, the planning, the registry of gifts—all followed inexorably but somehow insubstantially, like scenes constructed from pixels. A.G. sat in his car in the driveway and tried, at this late hour, to reconnect himself to this series of events. He knew he should feel elated, or scared—or both. He listened for the chuffing sound of the ocean waves. He wondered why you could always hear the surf from the yard at night but never during the day.

A rabbit rocketed across the driveway and disappeared into the privet, closely pursued by Woofter, the Keirsteads' retriever. The dog barked twice at the hedge before turning away and trotting back toward the house.

Leaving the Meadow Club after her tennis lesson, Ginny Banks caught a glimpse of a scene she'd never expected to witness: the rehearsal dinner for A.G.'s wedding. She stood at the edge of the doorway, looking in on the assembled company. Besides family, there was the table of best men—A.G. having assembled a team of five, rather than leaving anyone out. Tommy Briggs, Wick Seward, Nikos Menzenopolus, Cappie Farquarson and Gino Andreosa. Back in the day, they had all been known as ladies' men. Nikos and Gino were among the last of the old-school playboys in the mold of Agnelli and Rubirosa, race car-driving Euro sybarites. All of them had eventually married at least once—most of them twice, although Gino and Wick were currently between. They'd chased, and bedded, many of the same girls, initially women their own age and later their younger sisters. A.G. was the last of his kind, the last unmarried man of his generation. For two decades he had been a kind of prince of the city, gliding between the social clubs of the Upper East Side and the nightclubs downtown, an intimate of artistic circles as well as the world of inherited wealth. He belonged to the Racquet Club, the Brook Club and the Century Club, was an early investor in a famous SoHo art galley and a patron of several literary magazines. He was also a famous lover, a playboy who cut a wide swath through Manhattan and Europe, faithfully alternating between models and debutantes. For years he conducted an affair with a married screen idol, while continuing to pursue an international serial-dating career. His fortieth-birthday celebration, which took place on Nikos Menzenopolus's yacht, *Dionysus,* inevitably appeared on subsequent lists of "Parties of the Decade." Cappie Farquarson went into rehab three days later, and Nikos eventually became involved in two paternity suits, both plaintiffs citing A.G.'s party as the date of conception. A.G. himself managed to escape these kind of entanglements, although at some point in the years that followed his name began to be invoked as a synonym for a certain kind of arrested development. He'd been eligible for so long that he ceased to be plausible. Married couples, seating their dinner parties, began to think of him as a hopeless case—a quaint relic of their wild youth. "Who can we put next to Celia?" "There's always A.G." "Do we really want to do that to Celia? I mean, even if she hasn't already slept with him, I think she's had enough of the bad boys for one lifetime."

Ginny turned, to see Lori Haddad with her daughter Casey in tow, looking in on the scene. "Can you believe this?"

"I'm actually seeing it," Lori said, "but I still don't believe it."

"What don't you believe, Mommy?"

"He's still got twenty-four hours to leave the country."

"Maybe we're being too cynical."

"Mom, what don't you *believe* in?"

"Mommy doesn't believe in fairy tales, honey."

"What do you suppose it is about *her*? I mean, is it just that she happened to be the one sitting in the chair next to him when the music stopped?"

"Well, besides that she's young and pretty and thin and rich. And she's from his hometown. That seems to count for a lot with these southerners."

"Good point. So what does she see in him?"

"Well . . . He's charming and smart and he has a D-I-C-K the size of Florida."

"That sp—"

"We know what it spells, honey," said Lori, covering her daughter's mouth.

A. G. Jackson had grown up on Lookout Mountain in Chattanooga, although his own father was an émigré from Birmingham, by way of Vanderbilt. As the vice-president of the local bank, he was a respected member of the community, although their circumstances were more modest than those of the native oligarchy. A. G. distinguished himself as both scholar and athlete, joined his schoolmates on bonefishing expeditions to Islamorada and quail-hunting jaunts at their south Georgia plantations while his father managed their trust funds. A.G. was raised to believe there was no higher title a man could aspire to than "gentleman," and this episcopal epithet was so constantly attached to Jackson *père*, often accompanied by the adjective *old school*, that his son couldn't help but sense an almost imperceptible undercurrent of condescension from those whose secret faith was more Darwinian. The old man's rectitude was in part a reaction to the flamboyance of his own father, who'd made and lost two fortunes, one in stock speculation and one in real estate, while he was growing up. A.G.'s father did all he could to temper his son's fearless and exuberant character, so reminiscent of his grandfather's, while his wife secretly undermined this program, instilling in him a sense of confidence and entitlement. Her own family was among the first families of Charleston and she saw no reason to defer to the local gentry. Her husband would scold her for saying, as she so often did, "Who's the handsomest, smartest little man in the whole wide world?" "Please, Kate," he'd say. "You'll spoil the boy." While A.G. absorbed from his father a respect for tradition, position and inherited wealth, his mother taught him to believe in his own secret superiority. Their marriage, from his vantage point, was a happy one, although his mother sometimes believed that she'd sold herself short, that her husband lacked the necessary fire and grit to advance her ambitions.

No family loomed larger in Chattanooga than the Kiersteads. They had made their original fortune in land and later compounded it with an interest in a soft-drink empire based in Atlanta. In the past half-century their holdings had spread from the southeast throughout the country and around the globe. A.G. had gone to school with Burton Kierstead III, aka Trip, whose father had taken a benign interest in A.G.'s career, even writing him a letter of recommendation to Harvard. They had stayed in touch after A.G. moved to New York, occasionally dining together when Kierstead was in the city, and the old man sometimes steered some business his way. As a young investment banker, it certainly didn't hurt to be acquainted with Burton Kierstead, Jr. Trip, meanwhile, married a girl from Savannah, built a house on Lookout Mountain and took an office downtown, next door to his father's, which he visited when he wasn't following the salmon from Nova Scotia to Russia, or the birds from Georgia to Argentina. Their friend Cal Bustert, to nearly no one's surprise, burned through his trust fund, bouncing between fashionable resorts and rehab facilities; marrying, spawning and divorcing; wrecking cars and discharging firearms at inappropriate targets, including, finally, himself. A.G. had flown south for the funeral, a somber yet lavish affair that lasted for three days.

Most of their former classmates, after forays into the North, settled within a few miles of their parents and married girls they'd known for years. A.G. always returned for the weddings—five of them the year he turned thirty— and always brought a different date, and in time returned to stand as godfather to the children. He visited his parents on Thanksgiving and Christmas. Only rarely did he bring a girl along for these family holidays, and when he did, she was inevitably from what he called, without self-consciousness, "a good family." But his parents learned in time not to get too attached to any of them.

Despite his increasing success in New York, he maintained a deep loyalty to his hometown. Chattanooga, Tennessee, the South—this was part of him, and distinguished him from the mass of rootless Yankees with whom he associated in Manhattan. He always told his drinking buddies in both cities that he would return one day, although as the years passed it became harder and harder for his friends in either place to take this threat seriously.

Within a few years he was making more money than his father, although he did not announce this fact—except to his mother—and continued to seek his father's advice on matters large and small, although they did not discuss A.G.'s love life.

Ginny was reading in the living room of the little cottage in Sagaponack she rented every August, half-conscious of the wistful susurration of the waves from the beach. The shack, which had once enjoyed unobstructed views of the potato fields, had over the years been hemmed in by houses, first by Lego-like boxes and later by vast shingled mansions that mimicked the old cottages of Southampton, but at night she could still imagine herself as a lonely beachcomber. Emma Wodehouse was just realizing how badly she had misjudged both Mr Knightley and her own heart, when the phone rang, startling her. She was hardly less startled by the identity of the caller.

"A.G.?"

"Sorry to call so late. But I know you've always been a night owl."

"If you're looking for my niece, she's gone off to sleep over at a friend's house."

"No, actually I was looking for you. Wanna get a drink?"

"Now? Tonight?" Her watch said 1:45.

"We're not getting any younger."

"Don't you have a big day tomorrow?"

"That's probably exactly why I want to drop by."

She paused. She knew, of course, that she was going to say yes, but it irritated her that she was so pleased at the prospect of his coming over. Naturally, he was drunk and probably high. She'd been the recipient of many such late-night phone calls back in the day. She couldn't help feeling an illicit satisfaction in the fact that she was, after all these years, getting another, and on this of all nights. He was probably just feeling sentimental in his cups, but whatever his motivation, she had unfinished business with A. G. Jackson, and this might well be her last chance to close the account.

He was flushed, and his speech, always slower and more elided than that of his northern peers, was just a little slurrier than usual. But for all the nights they'd partied till dawn, she'd never really seen him lose control of his faculties.

He hugged her just a little longer and harder than he might have in a public encounter. "Hey, little darlin'. I can't tell you how glad I am to see you." She pointed him toward the living room couch. He set up camp on the couch and proceeded to lay out a pile of coke on the coffee table. "You don't mind, do you? I just need to settle my nerves."

"Oh, that should definitely do the trick," she said. "You're *so* mellow on coke."

"Well, you know. Old habits die hard."

Though it had been years since she'd done blow herself, it seemed perfectly normal to watch him chopping lines, since that's what they'd always done. Being transported back a decade wasn't such a bad thing for a girl. Plus, she was morbidly fascinated with his recklessness on the eve of his wedding. She couldn't help wondering just how far he would push it.

"Is that how you'd describe me? 'An old habit'?"

"I'd describe you as an old . . . a *close* friend." He laid out four identical lines with his SoHo House membership card. He always prided himself on this little skill.

She sat down beside him and accepted the rolled-up twenty. Always the gentleman, letting her go first. She felt a thrill of recognition as he held her hair back while she leaned over the table. And then the other familiar thrill, the chilly tingle in her sinuses that turned warm as it spread out toward the follicles of her scalp.

"Feels like old times," he said.

"Not exactly," she said.

"I can't believe it's been . . . God, how long *has* it been?"

"Seven years."

"No way."

"Yup."

"Well, it's not like we haven't seen each other around town."

"No, though you probably would have preferred me to just disappear into thin air."

"Oh, come on, darlin'. Don't be ridiculous. I'm always happy to see you." He leaned over and snorted his two lines.

"You weren't so happy to see me today at the beach."

"Well, that wasn't my best moment."

"So you admit you were hitting on my niece."

"It's a reflex. What can I say, she's a very pretty girl."

"I understand that. What I don't understand is tomorrow."

"Yeah, well. I'm not so sure I do, either."

"Don't you think you'd better figure it out?"

"I hardly think there's time for that," he said.

"Are you in love with her?"

"I suppose so. I'm not sure."

"Have you ever been in love?"

He nodded his head and looked off through the bay window, out across the invisible ocean, his eyes turning glassy. She realized with a start that he was on the verge of tears. When she slid across the couch and embraced him he virtually collapsed in her arms. "Once," he said.

At Harvard, A.G. had fallen in love with Eve Garrigue, who was a class ahead of him and who, by the time they met, had already published several poems in *The Paris Review*. He was aware of her legend—brainy, beautiful and hard-drinking—even before he arrived on campus, and he already knew her family, from New Orleans, in the way that all southerners know one another. A.G. had discarded his virginity at fifteen and never looked back. At first she found his boundless self-confidence absurd—a freshman wooing the most popular woman in the sophomore class—but eventually it won her over. He was precocious intellectually as well as sexually, and he was also a willing student. He wrote her a sonnet cycle, twelve strictly constructed love poems modeled on Wyatt's and Shakespeare's. And there was the tribal connection—they had a common set of cultural references and a common enemy in the subtle prejudice of all those who assumed that a southern accent was a sign of slow-wittedness.

Under Eve's influence, A.G. began to write poetry in the runic, oracular manner of Merwin and Strand; her own was high-pitched and baroque, reminding some of late Plath. Eventually he gave up verse, after realizing that he was a better critic than a poet, and a lesser poet than his girlfriend. He would provide the intellectual framework for her creation. In fact, he would've done almost anything for her. Accustomed to being intellectually and emotionally dominant, he happily acceded to her whims and opinions. He started smoking Gauloises and briefly abandoned the preppy wardrobe of his youth in favor of colorful long-collared shirts and flared pants. Eve, who had a breathtaking figure to show off, hid it beneath drapey vintage dresses and scarves. His devotion was extreme; he couldn't believe his luck in finding, so early in life, all the answers to his desires in one woman. They shared a destiny. While they gathered around them a group of friends and admirers, they were often criticized for being a universe of two.

They spent their second summer together backpacking in Europe; her family had offered to pay for a deluxe version of the grand tour, but Eve refused their money on principle. They bought Europasses and stayed in youth hostels, dined on bread and cheese and *vin du pays* and screwed like minks. By day they retraced the lives of the poets and sought out ancient churches. One afternoon in the cool, musty interior of a Romanesque church near Saint Paul de Vence, Eve knelt down on the stone floor and gave him a blow job. It was the most shocking thing that had happened to him in his life, though he didn't say anything, more fearful that she'd think him prudish and stop before she finished than he was of discovery or blasphemy.

They worried about what to do after graduation, which would come a year earlier for Eve. Marriage was discussed, but they agreed—or rather, Eve assured him—that they didn't believe in it. Finally she decided to go to Columbia for her master's. She'd take the four-hour train ride to see him every weekend, and in the meantime she could scout out Manhattan, a territory they planned to conquer together. Her senior year, Eve was invited to be a Fellow at Bread Loaf. A.G., interning in Chattanooga at a law firm, couldn't understand the diminishing volume and ardor of her letters and phone calls. She herself was almost impossible to reach. Frantic, he drove one Friday night from Chattanooga to Vermont, arriving at the mountain outpost of literature sixteen hours later, just in time to find a tousled Eve walking to breakfast, hand in hand with a middle-aged poet A.G. recognized from dust-jacket photos. Her surprise turned almost immediately to defiance. A.G. punched the poet, knocking him down. Eve jumped on his back and scratched his face as a small crowd of aspiring writers looked on.

In his young man's heart he believed he could never forgive her, but she astonished him by refusing to ask him to. Back in Chattanooga, he waited for the letter or the call, in his mind conducting the dialogue she refused to initiate. How could she? After all that time, after all they'd been through together. For all his intelligence and eloquence, the sentiments and even the words were the same as those of all spurned lovers. He spent hours engaged in this furious debate, but his side amounted to the repetition of a simple question: "How could you stop loving me?" This was his first experience of rejection. He had never been in love before, and some of his friends wondered if he ever would be again.

At his father's insistence, A.G. had taken half a dozen economics classes already, and having finished most of his course work in English, he decided to do a double major in literature and economics. He took up with a new set of friends, avoiding most of those he and Eve had known. He had no idea what he wanted to do. After graduation he went to China to teach English, which he envisioned as a kind of romantic exile. The following year he enrolled in business school, and then, after a grueling year as an analyst at an investment bank, he found his calling as a closer—the guy who entertained the clients and held their hands as they signed the checks.

"So she broke your heart and drove you to banking?"

"I don't suppose it was quite that simple. I've probably simplified it in retrospect. Mythologized it in my mind."

"So how does this lead us to the present? To your imminent nuptials?"

He shook his head and chopped up more coke. "I don't know. I guess it just seemed like time." He folded the coke and chopped it again.

"That's it? It 'seemed like time'?"

He shrugged. "She's a nice girl, from a good family. You know, we have a lot in common. So, what about you?"

"What about me?"

"Have you ever been in love?" He was rubbing his face as if to wash off a spot—a tic that was terribly familiar to her.

"Once," she said, taking a cigarette from his pack and holding it to her lips while he lit it.

"Tell me about it."

"You know most of the story," Ginny said. "You were there."

"I was there?" He seemed determined to be obtuse.

"You were the one."

"Jesus. Are you—"

"Yes, I am serious. All those years, all those nights. I couldn't help it. I knew it was supposed to be fun, but I fell in love with you."

"I didn't know."

"You don't remember the last night we spent together?"

"Not exactly."

"You asked me to marry you."

"I did?" He looked horrified.

"You did. You asked me to marry you and you told me you wanted me to have your babies. We stayed up all night planning our future. We were going to spend our summers in Provence. And the next day you said you'd come to my parents' house for Thanksgiving. But later that same day you said you had a late meeting on Wednesday and you would take the train up to Bedford

Thursday morning. And that was the last I ever heard from you."

He slumped back on the couch. "That was terrible, really the worst—I know. I just didn't know what to say to you." He leaned forward and snorted another line. "I was going to go up to Bedford. Except I went out for a drink that night. And I met a girl. And one drink led to another. And the next thing I knew, it was noon the next day and we were finishing the last of the coke. I couldn't very well face your family in that condition. And, you know, letting you down like that . . . I knew I needed to call and apologize, but somehow I couldn't."

Well, at least now she knew what had happened. She bent over the coffee table and snorted another couple of lines. "It used to kill me to see you at parties," she said finally, "and you acting so casual, as if nothing had happened. With some babe on your arm. For a long time I hated you."

"I guess I can't really blame you," he said. "I wish there was some way—"

"Make love to me," Ginny said. In her own mind, she wasn't being sentimental so much as practical. She felt he owed her that much at least. Either it would be as good as she remembered it or it wouldn't, and she would've gotten it out of her system.

Up in the bedroom, he was smart enough, or considerate enough, to kiss her long and hard before he began removing her clothes. In the middle, for all his skill, and all her desire to be transported, she began to come back to herself and feel awkward and sad. And after what seemed like a very long time, she just wanted him to finish. She realized now that what she'd really wanted was to believe that he still wanted her and that he cared enough for her to betray his future wife.

Afterward, she wrapped herself in the bedspread and walked out to the deck. The sky had turned gray in the east and the dark surface of ocean was stippled with silver sunlight. The coke was wearing off, and her eyeballs felt as if they were being pricked with tiny needles. She hated herself.

Eventually, A.G., in his paisley boxer shorts, holding a cigarette, joined her on the deck.

"What are you going to do?" she said.

"I don't know." He took a drag. "Probably the correct thing."

"What's the correct thing?"

"It's what we do when we don't know what the right thing is."

He put his arm around her and held his cigarette to her lips. She inhaled greedily, as if she believed the smoke could save her, the ember blazing and crackling between A.G.'s fingers before it faded and dimmed within a cocoon of gray ash and he tossed it away, the last sparks dying on the dewy lawn below.

A NOTE ON THE AUTHOR

Jay McInerney came to prominence in 1984 with his first novel *Bright Lights, Big City*. He is the author of six further novels—*Ransom, Story of My Life, Brightness Falls, The Last of the Savages, Model Behaviour* and *The Good Life*—the collection of stories *How It Ended* and, most recently, a work of non-fiction, *A Hedonist in the Cellar*. He lives in New York City.

A NOTE ON THE TYPE

The text of this book is set in Adobe Garamond. It is one of several versions of Garamond based on the designs of Claude Garamond. It is thought that Garamond based his font on Bembo, cut in 1495 by Francesco Griffo in collaboration with the Italian printer Aldus Manutius. Garamond types were first used in books printed in Paris around 1532. Many of the present-day versions of this type are based on the *Typi Academiae* of Jean Jannon cut in Sedan in 1615.

Claude Garamond was born in Paris in 1480. He learned how to cut type from his father and by the age of fifteen he was able to fashion steel punches the size of a pica with great precision. At the age of sixty he was commissioned by King Francis I to design a Greek alphabet. For this he was given the honourable title of Royal Type Founder. He died in 1561.